WICKED

Wicked

Pepper McGraw

CONTENTS

PEPPER MCGRAW

Twins.

One whose magic is rigid and constrained, the other's a hurricane of chaos.

Samantha Covington has always believed that order and restraint are the most important ingredients to a happy and safe existence. She prides herself on her absolute control and if that control somehow messes with her ability to cast the perfect spells, well, so be it. Better an organized life than one of utter chaos like her twin's.

Sadly, when her mother loses patience with the twins' inability to control their magics and casts a spell to infect Samantha with a bit of her sister's spontaneity, Samantha's life is suddenly a whole lot less controlled. Especially when she's around Jack Saunders, a man whose sheer masculinity has always tempted her to recklessness. Now Samantha's in a battle, not just against the chaos her mother has cursed her with, but also against her own sexuality, which seems to have wakened with a ferocity she's never before experienced.

How in all the chaotic realms will her ordered life survive the likes of Jack Saunders?

Chapter One

"WHAT DO YOU think she wants?" Samantha muttered to her twin sister, Serena, as they waited for their mother, Elizabeth, to get off the phone with one of the department managers.

Serena sighed. "Probably wants to lecture us again."

Samantha refrained from rolling her eyes, though she desperately wanted to. "It *is* that time of year, I suppose."

"You'll both be thirty soon," Serena whispered, sounding remarkably like their mother.

"It's past time for the two of you to gain control of your magic," Samantha whispered back.

"Work together," Serena said.

"Stop arguing," Samantha said.

"Learn from each other," the two of them chorused in soft tones.

"Right. That's quite enough," Elizabeth snapped.

"Oops," Samantha muttered.

"Obviously the two of you know exactly why I've called you into my office, so I won't bother with the lecture this time."

That was unexpected. And purely wondrous.

Samantha envisioned giving Serena a high five and knew from the tingling in the palm of her hand that Serena had high-fived her back.

"So if you know what I'm going to say, why haven't the two of you managed to figure things out yet?" Elizabeth demanded.

"There's nothing to figure out," Samantha said. "We're just too different."

"Exactly," Serena said. "Samantha's too serious and—well—"

"Serena's too reckless," Samantha said.

"I wouldn't put it quite that way, but—" Serena paused a moment, then corrected herself. "Actually, yes, I would, but I like the chaos that comes from recklessness."

"And I like being in control," Samantha said. "Honestly, giving up my magic to achieve that control is a small price to pay. Much better not to use my magic at all than to be a victim of its chaos like Serena."

"I wouldn't say I'm a victim." Serena grinned. "More like a conspirator."

"Don't be ridiculous," Elizabeth said. "You two are twins, which means you have double the potential of any other witch. Triple it even."

Serena groaned. "Mother, the twin amplification effect is just propaganda."

"And even if it isn't, it's not worth the risk," Samantha said. "You've seen some of Serena's castings. Now imagine if we *did* achieve synchronicity and my powers actually amplified hers. I can't even imagine the chaos that would result. Restraining my magic really is for the best."

"I disagree entirely," their mother said. "And not gaining control of your magic has real world consequences. Neither one of you will be earning a place on the Board of Directors at this rate."

Serena made a scoffing sound. "As if I'd want to sit on a Board full of stodgy old witches."

Samantha scowled. "I've already come to terms with losing that possibility, Mother. I really don't need to be reminded over and over again."

Serena whirled to stare at Samantha. "Are you saying you *want* to be on the Board?"

Samantha shrugged. "It's not possible so I prefer not to think about it."

Serena groaned. "Look, if I knew how to help you, I would. But your magic is too—" she made fists with her hands and shook them "—rigid and constrained. It allows for no flexibility at all. I have no idea how to work with it."

"Yes, and your magic is like a hurricane that never stops. It causes chaos everywhere."

Serena shrugged a shoulder. "I like chaos."

"I know." Samantha sighed. "But it doesn't help when we're casting from the same well."

"Yes, and it's time for both of you to gain control of that well," Elizabeth said.

"My half is under perfect control," Samantha said.

Elizabeth sighed. "Not accessing the well isn't the same as controlling it, Samantha. In fact, you're so locked down, I'm concerned your magic won't respond in an emergency situation."

Again, this was a risk Samantha was willing to take.

"And you, Serena, your magic is always on the verge of explosion. You could learn some restraint from your sister while Samantha could learn a bit of spontaneity from you."

"I'm not really interested in learning spontaneity, Mother," Samantha said.

"Nor am I interested in gaining any restraint," Serena said. "That doesn't sound fun at all."

"Yes, well, I'm afraid you're both out of luck."

"What?" Samantha and Serena chorused.

"Here's the deal. I considered the merits of the whole body switching thing, but that's so cliche and overdone, so instead, a little bit of Serena's recklessness to you—" She flicked her fingers at Samantha, who jolted as what felt like static electricity ran through her entire body. "—and a little bit of Samantha's restraint to you." She flicked the fingers of her other hand at Serena, who jumped in her chair and looked terribly spooked.

"Mother, what did you just do?" Samantha asked.

"I've shared a bit of your sister's personality with each of you. The more restrained you try to become, Samantha, the more reckless you will act. I'd suggest you loosen up a bit before you destroy the world. And as for you, Serena, the more outrageous your behavior, the less fun you will actually have."

"Hey." Serena leapt to her feet. "You can't do that. You can't dictate the amount of fun I get to have."

"Well, luckily for you both, the spell will only last for as long as necessary for you to learn control, Serena, and for you, Samantha, to learn to be spontaneous."

"I can't be spontaneous, Mother," Samantha exclaimed. "It goes against everything I believe in. Order, restraint, control. These are the bedrocks of a happy and safe life."

"Oh, Samantha." Serena sighed. "You really do need to loosen up, have a bit of fun, live a little. Safety has no value if you don't have a life to go with it." She turned and headed for the door.

"Where are you going?" Samantha exclaimed. Didn't she understand what their mother had done to them?

"I'm off to have some fun, of course. Good luck with those spells, Mother." She paused at the door to glance back at them. "I highly doubt there's a casting in existence that will accomplish your goals, but if it makes Samantha loosen up a bit and live a little, well, I guess I'm willing to restrain my fun, for a while at least." And on that note, she abandoned Samantha, leaving her alone to tackle the task of convincing their mother to take it all back.

An hour later, Samantha stormed into her office, frustrated and annoyed.

No amount of begging had convinced Elizabeth to undo the casting, which meant Samantha was still cursed.

And utterly doomed.

She expected the humiliation to be endless, especially if she ended up acting as recklessly as Serena.

If that happened, she might just have to leave the state. Start over somewhere entirely new. She supposed she could move to Jamesville. Her cousins were quite happy there, though she had no idea how they could stand to live among so many non-witches, and Aunt Dory would undoubtedly welcome her with open arms.

But her cousins, ugh.

Those three had what she and Serena had never been able to find. Synchronicity.

They were close, as close as sisters could be, and their magic was quite powerful as a result, which gave Samantha a brilliant idea.

She picked up the phone and called her oldest cousin, Megan.

After a fifteen-minute, extremely frustrating conversation, Samantha wanted to cry.

According to Megan, the type of casting Samantha described wouldn't be easily tampered with, and in fact, they could make things vastly worse by trying.

"So I'll just avoid people," Samantha said to herself while pacing around the room. "Yes. That sounds like a perfect plan. Avoid people and maybe everything will work out just fine."

"You do know that you're expected at the community center in an hour. And then there's the speech this evening at the fundraiser."

Samantha looked up at Meredith who stood in the door of her office. "What?"

"Community center. Fundraiser. Speech."

"Oh, dear sweet goddess of change. Save me."

"Huh?"

Samantha waved her arms in a flurry of movement. "Cancel it."

"What?"

"Cancel everything. Every appointment, every meeting, all of it. Canceled."

"Are you feeling all right?"

"Just cancel everything," Samantha exclaimed.

"Okay." Meredith looked a little stunned. "But what are we going to do about the community center, not to mention the fundraiser?"

"Give them to Jack. Make him go."

"But Jack drives you crazy."

"Exactly."

"You really want Jack to get all the press from the event?"

Samantha blanched at the thought of the press being witness to whatever recklessness her mother had unleashed on her. "Yes, absolutely. Just do it."

"All right. If you say so."

As soon as Meredith left, Samantha rushed back to her desk and collapsed in the chair there. What was she going to do? Become a hermit? Avoid humanity for the rest of her life?

She didn't want to learn how to be reckless. It would ruin everything. Her reputation. Her sense of self. The predictability of her days.

Chaos!

That's what she had to look forward to and she blamed Serena.

With a scowl, Samantha grabbed her phone and texted her sister. *This is all your fault.*

A kissing emoji appeared on her screen.

Unbelievable. Could Serena take nothing seriously? *I'm hiding out in my office because of you. Missing the community center event because of you.*

Her phone rang.

Samantha answered it with a growled, "What?"

"Are you seriously going to miss the community event you've spent months planning out of fear?"

"Of course I am. You heard Mother. Who knows what craziness might ensue if I go? What if I decide to go skinny dipping in a fountain or—or binge out on the taco bar?"

Serena burst into laughter. "First of all, is there even a fountain at the community center? I don't think so. And one good taco bar binge isn't going to ruin you. Besides, isn't the taco bar for the kids?"

"That's not the point," Samantha exclaimed. "The press will be there, Serena. I can't risk it."

"That right there, Samantha, is why Mother cast that spell in the first place."

"What do you mean?"

"Even I can see that you're only going through the motions. You don't have a life, Samantha. You're just marking time."

"I do so have a life. I'm very busy, I'll have you know."

"Of that, I have no doubt. But when was the last time you had fun, Serena?"

"Fun? I'm an adult. I do adult things. Fun is not a requirement."

Serena laughed. "Of course it's not a requirement, but it sure does make life interesting."

Chapter Two

"YOU'RE KIDDING ME." Jack stared at Meredith incredulously.

"I"m serious. She told me to cancel everything and to send you to the event."

"Is she sick?"

"I don't know. She definitely seemed off."

"All right. Thanks, Meredith." Jack glanced at the clock. If he was going to make it to the community center in time, he would have to leave in fifteen minutes. Just enough time to confront Samantha.

He had no idea what was going on, but this was highly unusual.

She wasn't exactly his favorite person on earth, mostly because she was all business and didn't seem to even notice the boiling attraction between them. Which frankly, he couldn't understand at all. How could she miss the sparks?

Still, annoying as he found her, he was a bit concerned at Meredith's news.

The Samantha he knew would never miss an event like this. It was worth its weight in good advertising.

He'd just reached Samantha's door when he heard her say, "Fun is not a requirement."

Jack rolled his eyes. Now *that* was the Samantha he knew.

Though, perhaps, not her exactly, since at the moment she was pacing back and forth, waving an arm wildly in the air as she spoke into her cell phone.

"What are we going to do, Serena?"

She paused in her pacing to gasp, then exclaim, "Well, that's easy for you to say. A little restraint can only improve your life. Recklessness, though, that's a recipe for disaster."

She listened some more, then said, "Well, thanks for nothing, Serena. I can tell the spell hasn't kicked in for you yet."

She let out an exasperated sound. "Fine." She whirled in her pacing, caught sight of Jack in the doorway and froze. "I have to let you go now, Serena. Yes, work calls. Uh-huh. Okay. Good luck." She ended the call and stared at Jack. "Why are you here?" She glanced down at the phone. "You need to get to the center."

* * *

Jack Saunders was the last man on earth Samantha would ever choose to witness her epic meltdown, but just her luck, he'd arrived in time to do just that. She could only pray he'd overheard very little of her conversation with her sister.

She hoped by ending the call and shooing Jack on his way that he would leave her to wallow in her misery.

Instead, he pushed away from the doorframe he'd been leaning on and walked toward her.

It should have gotten easier over time for Samantha to ignore the zing she felt whenever she was in his presence. Instead, it had only gotten more difficult, and today, with her emotions all over the place, it was practically impossible.

His sheer masculinity made the breath catch in her throat as he prowled toward her.

She spun on her heels, intending to put her desk between the two of them.

Somehow, though, she stumbled over her own feet and for a split second thought she was going to fall, but then Jack caught her in his arms.

"Careful there." He steadied her against him. "You okay?"

Samantha pressed her hands against his chest and pushed back. "Yes, thank you."

She glanced up and saw that a lock of his gorgeous, black hair had fallen into his eyes.

She lifted a hand, intending to brush the hair away, when she realized what she was doing.

It was happening already!

She fisted her hand and dropped it to her side, but somehow her other hand was there in its place, brushing aside his hair before she could stop it.

Her eyes widened and she tried to step back, but his hands were on her hips, holding her steady.

"What's going on, Samantha?" He stared down at her, one eyebrow lifted over gorgeous brown eyes.

She stared into them, half dazed at the close proximity to this man who had always made her feel a bit reckless.

Oh, no.

"Samantha?"

"Um. Nothing. Nothing. I just, I need to—um—I need to go. Yes. I—I have to go."

"We both do. So let's go, all right?"

"Yes." In a bit of a daze, Samantha grabbed her purse and briefcase and followed Jack out of the office. He led her to the elevator and they headed down to the garage. She didn't even protest when he led her to his truck and settled her in the passenger seat. It was only when they were on the street and clearly headed in the direction of the community center that she came back to her senses.

"Oh, I can't—I can't go. I need to—um. I can't go to the center. Too many people there. The press. Oh, goddess, the press. You can do the tour and the speech tonight and all the things. I need to go home or —or leave the country. Yes. That's it. Maybe just take me to the airport. Or no, that won't work. You have to go to the community center. You can't be late. So maybe drop me off here. Yes, here. I'll catch a cab. You go on to the center."

* * *

Jack had absolutely no idea what was going on, but he kind of loved it.

Samantha had avoided touching him since the day they'd met when she'd shaken his hand, then dropped it like a hot potato.

Now, in the span of about twenty minutes, he'd witnessed her in a tizzy on the phone with her sister, had caught her in his arms as she'd almost fallen off her heels (something he would have sworn even a day ago was an impossibility), had held her close as she'd brushed his hair out of his eyes, and now had her in his truck and was listening to her babble.

Samantha Covington. Babbling.

She was still babbling when they arrived at the center and he escorted her inside.

Then, of course, everyone converged on her, needing her for this crisis or that, and Jack couldn't believe the change that came over her.

Usually, he only joined the fundraiser at the dinner party which would take place across town in a ritzier area of the city. If he'd had to guess, he would have assumed that Samantha had never been to the community center except for publicity stunts, which now that he thought about it, didn't even make sense considering her family had pretty much built the center from the ground up.

Still, he was completely stunned as people at the center greeted Samantha by name and the teens and children in particular, greeted her with cheers and hugs.

Even more amazing was the smile on Samantha's face and the way her entire demeanor seemed to relax as each moment passed in the center.

"The dragon lady's actually human, after all."

Jack grinned. "Neil, good to see you."

"You too. I had no idea agreeing to cover this story for Joe would result in this." Neil stared as Samantha let out a joyous laugh, something Jack would have assumed wasn't even possible not ten minutes before. "Who would have believed it, huh?"

"Well, I always figured there had to be a bit of human inside her, even if it was buried deep," Jack said. "After all, this event wouldn't be so important to her otherwise."

Neil looked doubtful. "I figured she did it for the publicity and good will."

Jack nodded. "I kind of thought the same thing, but now that I think about it, she could probably pay for publicity outright and spend a lot less than she does on this event every year. I doubt the community center reimburses her for the money she spends on the front end."

"Well, it *is* her family's project, though word has it, it was really Samantha's idea and her family just went along for the ride."

"Really?"

"Yep."

Jack had always assumed the center was just a tax break for the very rich Covington family. Knowing it was Samantha's project from the beginning was rather surprising, given how privileged her roots were. It was proof, he figured, there was more to Samantha Covington than the outer shell she showed the world. His blood heated as she glanced over and gave him a tiny smile, almost as if she knew they were talking about her.

"Damn. She smiled at you." Neil sounded amazed, which pretty much matched how Jack felt.

"I have no idea what's going on with her today. She was completely insane earlier, babbling about needing to leave the country."

"What?"

"Yeah. I don't know. It was weird."

"Maybe she absconded with all the funds for the center," Neil suggested, his eyes lighting up with a reporter's glee.

Jack rolled his eyes. "Samantha Covington? That's who you're talking about, right? You think that woman has been engaged in—what, an embezzling scheme? From the community center she probably funds from her own pockets?"

Neil chuckled. "Okay. It *is* a little farfetched, but why else does somebody need to leave the country?"

"With Samantha, who the hell knows?"

They both laughed.

Chapter Three

SAMANTHA HAD THE weirdest feeling Jack and Neil were talking about her. No matter where she went or who she was speaking with, she could feel Jack's eyes on her, following her around the room. It made her flustered.

It took a while to calm everyone down and get them to their stations throughout the center. It seemed everyone wanted to speak with her today, which wasn't necessarily unusual, though she felt more self-conscious with Jack's wickedly heated gaze following her everywhere.

Finally, it was time to meet the press, which meant shooing Neil outside where the rest of the press was waiting—she had no idea who had let him in, but she was betting all he'd had to do was bat those baby blue eyes and any of the center's residents, male or female, would have let him inside. Of course, approaching Neil meant approaching Jack again.

That was okay, though, because she was counting on Jack to deal with the media.

She strode toward them with as much confidence as she could muster when she felt unusually flustered.

Damn her mother. And damn Serena too.

"Jack, I need you to handle the press outside, and you, Neil, need to head outside as well. Tour doesn't start for another five minutes."

Neil grinned. "Aw, come on, Samantha. You know you want to give us a private tour." He waggled his brows at her, which made her blush.

Unbelievable!

"Go on now. Out you go. And you with him, Jack." She started to turn away, but Jack caught her hand in his.

"Not without you, darling." He swung her into his side and slid an arm around her shoulders. "Lead the way, Neil."

With a grin, Neil headed for the front doors and Samantha, well and truly caught, had no choice but to move when Jack did.

Five minutes later, they were outside facing the press. Normally, Samantha had a long speech prepared for this moment.

Okay, she'd had one this morning as well.

Unfortunately, every single word had been obliterated by the curse of recklessness and the incredible sensation of being held close to Jack's side.

"Jack," she whispered. "I really can't talk to them."

He grinned down at her. "Don't worry, darling. You'll do great." And he nudged her right up to the podium, forcing her into the spotlight.

Dear goddess of order, please bring her composure back.

Samantha cleared her throat. "Welcome to all of you."

The soft buzz of conversation died down as everyone turned to face the podium. Samantha recognized most of the faces in the crowd. There were several reporters from local TV stations, as well as a few journalists from the local papers and some radio personalities as well. These were the people who truly cared about the community and who showed up every year to provide the center with much-needed publicity and to help with the fundraising efforts.

Samantha couldn't do all of this without them.

With that in mind, she began to speak.

* * *

Jack could tell by the surprised look on many of the reporters' faces that something different was happening today.

He wasn't sure exactly what it was, but there was a strain of emotion in Samantha's voice that he'd never heard before.

"Each of you are critical in the work that we do here. Not because you volunteer at the center or even because you're so rich that your funds keep our doors open."

A few chuckles from the crowd at the thought that reporters might actually get rich off their careers.

"Instead, what you do for this center, is priceless. You provide us a voice and an opportunity to share with the city the great works that we do here for the members of our community. We wouldn't get half the funding we do without your continual efforts on our behalf. Please know that we see you and your organizations and we do appreciate that you come year after year to celebrate with us and to share our story with the wider community. I know most of you have met her before, but I want to introduce the director of the center, Kerry Simmons, who will lead you on this year's tour. We're very excited to share our latest updates that came about from this past year's funding and each of your efforts on our behalf."

Samantha stepped back and waved Kerry forward, who began immediately to talk about the updates and programs that had been added since the previous year's fundraiser.

"See there?" Jack murmured when Samantha stepped back to his side. "That wasn't so bad at all, now was it?"

Samantha flashed him a startled look, then shrugged. "I suppose not."

* * *

In truth, Samantha couldn't remember a single word she'd spoken. She'd been in a bit of a panic and terrified that she would do something completely beyond the pale in front of the press.

She was simply grateful that she hadn't had the urge to strip naked or even worse, take Jack to the ground in a fit of passion.

Just imagining it sent a rush of wicked heat through her body. Clenching the day's program in her hand, she fanned herself desperately.

Kerry finished her brief speech and quickly organized the press into small groups, each with a couple teen volunteers assigned to lead them through the center.

As the final group headed around the building toward the playground at the back of the center, Samantha heaved a sigh of relief. Her part in this portion of the day's events was now over.

"Shall we?" Jack held out his arm.

Samantha hesitated, then tentatively placed a hand in the crook of his elbow and allowed him to escort her into the center.

The rest of the afternoon was uneventful, though Samantha felt as if disaster was just around every corner. It didn't help that she couldn't take her eyes off Jack.

To her surprise, he was incredibly popular with the children and teens at the center as he asked them questions and engaged them in conversation.

Even the most sullen of their teens seemed to perk up in his presence, vying for an opportunity to talk with someone they clearly looked up to. Since he'd admitted he'd never been to the center before, she could only guess it was his seemingly endless charm at work.

And then there was Neil. He'd gone off with another group, but from the occasional glimpses she caught of him, he had his own bevy of followers vying for his attention.

It was when one of the five-year olds tripped over a loose shoelace and fell to the floor, that Samantha realized she was in real trouble.

Jack beat her to Lexi and had her scooped into his arms, the deep rumble of his voice catching her attention and arresting her tears.

By the time Samantha reached them, Lexi was all smiles and Jack was too.

There was something about him cuddling sweet Lexi in his arms and looking so natural doing it, that made Samantha's heart rate pick up.

Handing the little girl off to her older brother, Jack turned to Samantha and winked.

A wave of heat rushed down her spine and she spun on her heels, intending to hurry away.

Except somehow her body overrode her mind and she swung back around, grabbed him by the hand and dragged him out of the main room and down the hall to the walk-in linen closet.

She jerked open the door and pushed him inside, followed him in and closed the door behind her. All the while, her brain was shrieking, "Abort, abort!" Hands on hips, she advanced on him. "What exactly are you doing?"

Jack looked a bit stunned. He glanced around at the shelves of towels and cleaning supplies, then back at Samantha. "Uh. I think that should be my question. What are *you* doing, Samantha? Not that I mind being dragged into a linen closet." He waggled his brows at her.

Samantha's heart gave a little leap and then began to race. Damn the man. He was messing with her equilibrium and taking total advantage. "My mother put you up to this, didn't she?"

Jack looked confused. "What are you talking about?"

"Oh stop acting so innocent. You're taking advantage of the reckless curse."

"The reckless—"

"You need to stop being—" She waved her arms in the air.

"Being what?"

"So very much you!"

Jack grinned at her.

That freaking sexy grin again. She just couldn't take it.

"And who exactly am I supposed to be if not me?"

Samantha growled low in her throat, then lunged at him.

She caught him by the lapels, dragged him down and kissed him.

Heat spiraled through her and then Jack took over the kiss.

He backed her against the door, leaned into her and utterly ravaged her mouth.

Only the door and his hands on her hips kept her from sinking to the floor in a puddle of goo.

Long, wicked moments later, he pulled away from her mouth to trail a line of kisses across her check and down her neck, then back up again.

"Damn," he muttered in her ear, bringing her back to her senses.

She pushed against his chest, trying to get a bit of space between them, trying desperately to catch her breath and to think for a moment. Dear goddess, everything was spiraling out of control, most especially her own emotions and actions. What had she been thinking, dragging this utterly scrumptious man into a linen closet with her? She was supposed to be avoiding him, not attacking him.

"I have to go." She pushed him back and reached for the doorknob behind her. "I have to get back out there, but—" She caught a breath at the thought of everyone seeing her in this state of agitation. "Do I look okay?" She reached up and patted at her hair, then smoothed down her shirt. She looked down at herself, but couldn't tell if she was put together enough to fool the press and anyone else who saw her.

And what if someone saw her exiting the closet? What if someone had seen her dragging Jack *into* it? This was a nightmare.

Jack chuckled. "You look beautiful, as always." He reached out a hand and tucked a lock behind her ear.

Samantha's breath hitched in her throat as she stared up at him. God. He was just so— "No. This, this right here is what I'm talking about." She waved an arm through the space between them. "You need to stop it. Stop acting so damn sexy." And she stormed out of the closet.

It wasn't until she'd reached the main room that she realized she hadn't even looked first to be sure no one was in the hall to see her exiting the linen closet.

She was utterly doomed.

* * *

Jack stared at the linen closet door as it slammed behind Samantha's retreating form, then grinned.

"Damn."

He just hadn't seen that coming at all.

But now that he had Samantha's taste on his tongue and seared into his memory banks, now that he'd experienced her passion, there was nothing that would keep him from claiming her as his own.

He was fully invested now.

Samantha Covington's days as a single witch were numbered.

Chapter Four

THE REST OF the afternoon at the center, Samantha avoided even looking at Jack.

Anytime he appeared in a room she was in, she darted to a different part of the center.

When the press had all left and it was time to head back to the office, Samantha caught a ride with a volunteer so that she could avoid being trapped in a truck again with the delectable Jack.

Upon arriving at the offices, she didn't even bother going in. She simply hurried to her car and headed for home. It wasn't like she was expected to show up and work between the two events, even though she usually did.

Today though, she called Meredith to give her a few last-minute instructions and to let her know she was heading home and would see her at the dinner event later that evening.

As she bustled around, getting ready for the event, Samantha put together a list of rules she needed to follow that evening.

Perhaps even for the rest of her life.

Or at least until her mother's castings wore off.

Rule number one was avoid Jack. Every other rule wasn't really necessary as long as she followed rule number one. Still, she should probably come up with a couple contingency rules, just in case.

By the time Samantha stepped into the shower, she had her list ready to go and recited it as she showered and dressed.

Avoid Jack.

Don't talk to Jack.

Don't look at Jack.

Especially don't look in his sexy eyes.

And no ogling his amazing body.

And no dancing.

Definitely no dancing with Jack.

She was so focused on her list of must-dos and must-nots that she was actually late leaving her apartment.

Okay, so she wouldn't really be late for the event. She was scheduled to arrive an hour before it started, just to make sure everything was set up and ready to go.

Of course, she *usually* arrived three hours early give or take, because everything had to be perfect.

This time, though, she would only be there about ninety minutes early, which okay, was still earlier than she was expected, but definitely not as early as she'd planned, which meant she was late.

She, Samantha Covington, was *late.*

Unheard of.

What was even more unheard of, though, was the sight that greeted

Samantha when she entered the hotel's event center.

Serena. Standing in the lobby, waiting for her.

"What?" Samantha stared at her sister in stunned amazement. "I don't understand." Serena usually showed up after dinner and all the speeches were over, just in time for the drinking and dancing. She'd literally *never* showed up for an event on time, let alone early.

"I know," Serena snarled. "I was bored okay?"

Samantha didn't think she'd ever heard her sister say those words in all her life. "Are you serious right now?"

"Completely. I blame Mother. I can't believe she did this to us."

"Well, I'm just glad you're here. We could really use the help getting everything set up."

Serena groaned, but followed Samantha to the ballroom and over the next hour, was right there, at Samantha's side, helping with every issue that came up.

Samantha was stunned and quite frankly, impressed.

Of course, the minute the guests began to show up, Serena abandoned Samantha in favor of flirting.

Samantha rolled her eyes and got back to work.

So far, setting up for the event had been a lot less stressful than usual.

Samantha wanted to think it was because Serena was there to help.

Unfortunately, she was afraid it was because her sense of order and perfection had been somehow damaged by the spell.

She found to her utter horror that she actually didn't care if the centerpieces were perfectly centered or not.

Nor did she obsess over the placement of the silverware.

She also hadn't insisted on straightening a single worker's tie or taste testing a single dish.

She'd mostly spent her time congratulating the workers on a job well-done.

They'd all looked perfectly stunned. Not at the thank-yous for she'd always been generous with those, but at the lack of micromanaging.

She was feeling rather ill herself.

The goddess of order had clearly abandoned her and the only one left in her place was the goddess of chaos.

The end was surely at hand.

* * *

Jack arrived at the hotel, rather annoyed.

He'd planned to pick up Samantha and bring her to the event, but she'd already left by the time he arrived at her townhome.

He knew she was expected an hour early, so he'd arrived at her place ninety minutes before the start of the event, figuring he'd have no difficulty convincing her to ride with him.

He should have realized Samantha Covington would never be so pedantic as to arrive on time.

Knowing her, she'd probably been at the event center for hours by the time he'd left his house to head for hers.

Of course, he had no one to blame but himself.

Once again, he'd underestimated Samantha's sense of order and precision.

So he'd called Neil and was now heading into the hotel bar to meet him for a desperately needed drink before the event. He figured he might actually need more than one to dial back his irritation, which was an absolute must, seeing as tonight would require all his charm if he had any hope of getting Samantha on the dance floor.

And he was determined there *would* be dancing.

Of course, it wasn't exactly fair that he was irritated with her. After all, she hadn't known he was planning to pick her up, so it wasn't like she'd stood him up or anything. That didn't alleviate his sense of aggravation though. Especially since she'd sneaked out of the center before he could give her a ride back to the offices that afternoon.

Neil was late.

He came bustling in just as Jack was ordering a second whisky on the rocks.

"You're not going to believe it," Neil said as he pulled out a chair and settled across the table from Jack.

"What is it?"

"Serena's here."

Jack raised an eyebrow. "Isn't that unusual for her?"

"Definitely. She actually arrived before Samantha. Word has it Samantha arrived late."

"Not possible." Jack shook his head. "She'd already left the house when I stopped by ninety minutes before the event."

Neil gave him a pitying look.

"What?"

"Ninety minutes? You do realize Samantha Covington routinely arrives at every event three to four hours ahead of time."

"Seriously?"

"Oh, yes."

"But Samantha pays for an event planner."

Neil shook his head. "You have no idea what you're letting yourself in for, do you?"

Jack remembered the blazing heat of Samantha's kiss and grinned.

"I know exactly what I'm in for and it's not Samantha's infamous sense of precision and order."

The two men laughed at the phrase Samantha was known for spouting.

Thirty minutes later, when they stepped into the ballroom at the event center, Jack's eyes were immediately drawn to Samantha.

She was chatting with one of the catering staff and they were both smiling.

The caterer nodded, said something to her, then headed for the kitchen, leaving Samantha on her own for a brief moment.

Jack fully expected her to jump into motion and begin networking as she always tended to do at these events, but instead she simply stood in place quietly.

Jack cocked his head and stared.

She seemed different. More relaxed than he'd ever seen her at one of these events.

He'd just decided to take advantage, when a group of men blocked his view of Samantha as they stopped to chat with her.

Jack's eyes narrowed.

"Huh," Neil said. "Serena's acting quite subdued."

Jack glanced at Neil and followed his gaze to Samantha's twin sister, who was chatting with a couple businessmen.

Jack stared.

Though Serena was smiling and nodding, there was an awkwardness and hesitation to her body language that he'd never seen in her before.

"Plus Samantha's not running around like a crazy person."

Neil was right.

Usually, Samantha was in a tizzy by the time Jack arrived at the event and yet, all she'd done so far was stand in the same spot, smiling and chatting with anyone who approached. In fact, he couldn't believe he was thinking it, but frankly, she was *slacking off*.

Neil let out a bark of laughter. "Don't let her hear you say that."

Jack blanched. He couldn't believe he'd said that out loud.

Samantha would be horrified to think anyone perceived her in such a fashion. "To be clear, the only one who might say that about Samantha's behavior right now would be Samantha herself."

"True." Neil grinned.

Jack looked at Samantha again, then shifted his gaze to Serena, who was definitely acting out of character as well. "You don't think they switched—" He broke off. That didn't even make sense. They might be twins, but they certainly weren't identical. Plus he'd never felt attracted to Serena the way he was to Samantha.

"No way," Neil said. "If they had, Serena would be bustling around trying to fix everything."

"Yeah." Jack nodded. "And Samantha would be flirting with everyone in sight." He narrowed his eyes as she threw back her head and laughed at something a man said to her. *Was* she flirting? He let out a huff. "Gotta go, Neil."

Neil grinned. "Good luck."

* * *

Samantha was standing with a group of businessmen, nodding to what one of them was saying, when an arm slid around her waist and she inhaled Jack's deliciously masculine scent.

She'd already forgotten the very first rule!

"Sorry to interrupt," Jack said. "You ready to find a table, baby?"

What was he doing? "No. I—"

He grinned. "I'm sure Dave and the rest of these gentlemen will forgive me for stealing you away for a moment."

Dave chuckled. "Go for it, man."

Before she could even sputter out a protest, Jack had whisked her away from the group.

She was so busy reminding herself of all the rules—

Do not, whatever you do, look into his eyes.

Also, absolutely no touching.

Hold on, that ship had already sailed—

to notice where he was taking her.

Broom closet? What?

"What are we doing in here? How did we—where are we? There are no broom closets in the ballroom."

Jack grinned at her. "I thought we could celebrate our anniversary in here, relive our momentous first kiss."

"What anniversary? That was barely—" she glanced down at her phone and did a quick calculation. "—five hours ago!"

"Exactly. It's been entirely too long since our last kiss."

Samantha scowled at him, intending to demand he let her out of the broom closet immediately—there were so many things she should be doing—except in the process, she broke another rule. His sexy grin charmed her and before she knew it, she was gazing into his sexy eyes.

Oh, dear goddess of all sexy men, she was doomed.

She really needed to tell him no. She needed to demand out of this room. She needed to—

Kiss him.

Samantha had no memory of actually moving, but the next thing she knew, her legs were wrapped around Jack's waist with her dress somehow hiked around her hips, one of Jack's broad hands was plastered to her ass, the other was cradling her head, and they were kissing.

And oh, what a kiss.

Shivers wracked her spine as Jack plunged his tongue deep.

She needed him.

Right here. Right now.

She wrapped an arm around his shoulders and pulled herself up higher, trying desperately to get closer, to imprint herself on his very cells.

The world narrowed to Jack as a haze of desire obliterated all thoughts of the fundraiser and the long hours yet to come. Everything was gone in the blazing fire of his kiss.

A pounding sound intruded, but Samantha ignored it with a soft whimper.

"Samantha Covington! Are you in there? Open this door at once, young lady."

Jack let out a groan and Samantha whimpered again.

After one last, exquisitely long kiss, Jack lowered her to the floor, kissing every part of her he could reach on the way down.

She stepped back and quickly wiggled and pulled at her dress until it was finally positioned correctly. She ran a hand through her hair, a feeling of deep familiarity racing through her as she realized she was repeating motions she'd made earlier that day.

Jack stepped toward her and she flung up her hand in the universal stop sign.

"No, no, no," she hissed at him. "My mother is out there."

"Samantha. You need to open this door right now!"

Samantha raised an eyebrow at Jack, who grinned and shrugged. "I cast the room. No one can hear us or open the door. In fact, she can't possibly know we're here at all."

Samantha snorted. "You do *not* know my mother. She could find me in the middle of a clone convention surrounded by my own doppelgängers." She heaved a sigh. "We might as well get this over with."

"If you say so." Jack leaned over and kissed her on the cheek, murmuring in her ear, "You kiss like a dream, my sweet, stunning Samantha."

She froze at the words, the gentleness of his kiss, and the tenderness in his eyes.

Jack was so much more than she'd ever expected.

He waved a hand at the door and then opened it to Samantha's own personal hell.

Chapter Five

"SERIOUSLY, SAMANTHA, I cannot believe you," Elizabeth Covington lectured as they walked back toward the ballroom. "I count on you to be the reliable one. We're now fifteen minutes behind schedule because you're off hiding in a broom closet with Jack Saunders."

"Well, excuse me, Mother, but perhaps if you wanted reliability, you should have waited until after the event to toss recklessness my way."

"Hm." Elizabeth let out a huff of exasperation. "Well, I certainly didn't expect it to have such an immediate effect. For heaven's sake, Samantha, the community center depends on this fundraiser to not only keep its doors open but to ensure it remains in good condition."

Samantha rolled her eyes. "Mother, you know as well I do that all the prep work has been done. The people here tonight have already decided what they're going to donate and we'll happily take their pledges and checks." Even as she said the words, Samantha couldn't believe they were coming out of her mouth. They were words Serena spouted to her every year, trying to convince her to enjoy the event, rather than constantly working the attendees as if they might increase their intended donation based on her considerable networking skills.

Well, they might.

But for once, Samantha had other worries.

Like trying to avoid Jack—epic fail.

And also, trying to somehow avoid acting reckless in front of the elite of their city—fail again.

"Well, I guess we'll find out, won't we?" Elizabeth snapped.

What was she going on about now? "Find out what?"

"Whether or not your networking in the past has increased donations. Since you didn't bother this year, we'll see how our donations look at the end of the night." Elizabeth tossed Samantha an irritated look. "I'll be very disappointed if they're less than what we projected."

Samantha refused to feel guilty. "Well, if they are, Mother, you'll only have yourself to blame." And with that parting shot, Samantha stalked into the ballroom, where she sent a regal nod to the rather-stressed looking event manager, who immediately began barking orders at the catering staff.

"You know, if you'd let your event manager do the job she was hired to do, dinner would be on time right now." Serena slid into the spot at Samantha's side and smirked at her.

"Oh, please, not this again."

"I'm just saying. Why bother to hire an event manager if you plan on running the thing yourself?"

"I don't. She does all the things I'd rather not deal with. You know, the hiring and the decision-making and—"

"Uh-huh. And who approved the menu?"

Samantha scowled. "I did, but she put it together. I simply gave the final stamp of approval."

"And how many changes did you insist upon before approving it?"

"We needed a vegetarian option."

"I'm sure you did. But did you need three?"

Samantha gave a huff of exasperation. "Why is it that meat-eaters can have three options at a dinner, but when we try to give the same to vegetarians, it's appalling? I just don't understand your thinking. You do realize the diverse menu is what gets so many people in the door."

"Or perhaps they just want the tax break," Serena said.

"Or perhaps," Jack said as he came up behind them and slid an arm around Samantha from behind, "they care about the community center."

Serena looked stunned at the sight of the two of them together.

Rather like Samantha had been feeling all day—as if she'd been hit over the head by an anvil.

An anvil of lust.

"You two are together now?" Serena exclaimed. "When did this happen?"

Samantha sent her an exasperated look. "We're not together." She tried to discreetly remove Jack's hand from her waist, but he wouldn't be budged. "And when do you think?"

Serena's eyes widened and then she let out a hoot of laughter. "You are shitting me!"

"Serena!"

"I'm sorry, but this is awesome." Serena's shoulders shook with laughter. "I was really looking forward to seeing my sister dance in a fountain naked, but honestly, I think this is so much better."

"Dancing in a fountain naked?" Jack rumbled. "When is this happening and where?"

Samantha rolled her eyes. "That would be never. Why don't you go to your table, Jack? We need to get this show on the road."

"Oh, we're all up front together," Serena said.

"What?"

"Mother set it up. Something about the two of you and a broom closet. I didn't quite understand it, but she moved the Millers to a different table and Jack plus someone else to ours."

Jack grinned. "That's perfect. Remind me to thank your mother later."

This was not perfect at all. How could she possibly follow all of her rules if Jack was right next to her all night long?

"Well, come along then," she snapped and stalked toward the front, Serena and Jack following quietly behind.

As Samantha maneuvered between the tables, headed for theirs at the front, she went over the rules in her head.

It wasn't exactly a happy list.

So far, it seemed she'd broken them all.

Let's see.

Avoid Jack—fail.

Don't talk to Jack—epic fail.

Don't look at Jack and definitely don't look into his sexy eyes—impossible to follow.

No ogling of his amazing body—well, she hadn't exactly ogled it, more like attacked it. Perhaps that rule should be changed.

No attacking Jack's amazing body. A rule that *should* be easy to follow. Unfortunately, her body didn't seem interested in the commands her brain sent it.

That damn spell.

Oh and the last rule—no dancing.

This was a rule she hadn't yet broken!

All she had to do was stand strong.

Absolutely no dancing with the sexiest man she'd ever met.

That shouldn't be too difficult.

Right?

* * *

Jack couldn't take his eyes off Samantha. She was full of nervous cheer and received more than one surprised look as the night wore on.

At dinner, she charmed everyone at their table, making sure that everyone was a part of the conversation.

Neil, of course, was busy flirting with Serena, who Jack was amused to notice, didn't appear to be charmed at all. In fact, if he didn't know any better, he'd think she was giving Neil the cold shoulder.

Then it was time for the speeches, the one portion of the evening Jack always thought was the most boring. Except for once in her life, Samantha appeared to be approaching the podium without any notes. Or her phone.

"Is she just going to wing it?" Serena asked, a stunned look on her face.

Elizabeth, the twins' mother, looked equally concerned. "Surely not."

"Well, she did wing it at the press conference this afternoon," Neil pointed out. "She did quite fine actually. Short and to the point. I, for one, greatly appreciated it."

Serena gave an impertinent sniff. "You would."

Hm. Yes. Some definite tension there.

Jack raised an eyebrow at Neil, who just grinned.

It became clear as Samantha began to speak, that she wasn't, in fact, reading from a script. Nor, he suspected, had she memorized this particular speech.

Nope.

In fact, Ms. Samantha Covington seemed to be, well, *rambling* a bit.

In an adorable way, of course. Actually, she was rather eloquent and endearing and she got quite a few chuckles from the crowd.

"What in the world has gotten into your sister?" Elizabeth hissed at Serena.

Serena snickered. "I'm sure that's quite obvious, Mother. Really. It's all your fault. Casting recklessness willy-nilly."

Jack leaned forward. "What are you talking about?"

"Oh, didn't Samantha mention that our dear, sweet mother cursed us both?"

"Oh, don't be ridiculous, Serena. It isn't a curse to have a *bit* of decorum."

Serena rolled her eyes. "Well, how about a bit of no-fucks-given?"

"Serena!"

"What? Seriously, look at Samantha. She's clearly run utterly out of fucks." She waved a hand at her sister, who rather than giving her typical speech about the community center and its many efforts with the youth of the city, was instead sharing with the crowd a couple jokes the children had told her, as well as a few hilarious stories about the teens and their dramas.

"As you can see," Samantha said. "The center isn't simply a place for the people of the community to gather. It's a home-away-from-home, a sanctuary, a place where they know they will always be welcome and where they will always feel a sense of belonging. Thank you so much for being here tonight, to support the center and our efforts to keep it serving the community for a long time to come."

She stepped away from the podium and headed toward the stairs as a thunderous applause rose.

Jack stood and met her at the base of the stairs and escorted her back to their table. As he settled her back in her chair, he brushed a kiss across her cheek and murmured, "You were amazing."

She blushed.

Really, she was incredible. He'd had no idea she knew the people at the center so well.

"What on earth was that?" Elizabeth demanded. "What happened to the speech you've been writing for the last week and a half?"

Samantha shrugged. "I decided it was too boring. Who cares about statistics? It's the people the center serves who matter."

Elizabeth looked surprised. "Well, I don't disagree, but for heaven's sake, Samantha, you were babbling."

"Was I?"

Serena giggled. "A little. But no one seemed to mind. And the photos were a really nice touch."

Samantha nodded. "I'll have to thank Kerry and Meredith. Kerry gathered the photos and sent them off to Meredith, who put everything together. It was all very last minute."

"Well, it was quite well done."

The next hour or so was rather torturous as more speeches were given and the various courses were delivered.

Personally, Jack would have been thrilled to skip straight to the dancing portion of the evening, but then he would have missed the look on Samantha's face as she savored her chocolate mousse.

As she sucked every morsel of chocolate from the spoon, her eyes closed in bliss.

She wasn't even *trying* to seduce him, a fact that made the moment all the sexier.

Jack's temperature rose as she went for another bite, the sheer eroticism of her tongue licking the spoon making him growl.

Across the table, Neil let out a low rumble as well.

Jack jerked his eyes to his friend, ready to tear his head off, only to realize Neal's eyes were riveted to Serena, who was enjoying her own dessert.

Jack grinned.

Apparently the twins had more in common than they believed.

By the time dinner was done, speeches were given, and acknowledgements of benefactors made, Jack was unbearably impatient and desperate to hold Samantha in his arms.

The moment the music began, he was on his feet helping Samantha to hers.

She had a slightly dazed look on her face as he led her onto the dance floor.

What followed were hours of bliss as they danced the night away.

Of course, Samantha kept slipping away to speak with this person or that, but he always followed and always managed to coax her back onto the dance floor for just one more song.

A song that turned into as many as he could get away with.

And of course, whenever he could manage it, he maneuvered them into the shadows where he'd kiss her breathless, then spin her back out onto the dance floor for another turn.

* * *

Jack was an amazing dancer.

Perhaps if he weren't, Samantha would have been able to resist temptation.

Probably not though.

The man had ridiculous charm and was so damn sexy.

She found herself brushing his hair out of his eyes, seeking his form whenever she was pulled away for a conversation with someone else, and following his lead whenever they made it to the dance floor.

His kisses kept her heated all night long and the intensity of his eyes as he wooed her while dancing kept her unbalanced and trembling with need.

By the time the night had worn down, Samantha was a bundle of neediness, desperate for more than just his heated kisses.

"I'm heading out now," Serena said to Samantha when she and Jack returned to the table for a quick glass of water.

"Already?"

Serena never left the party early. Well, unless she was leaving *with* someone. Samantha grinned. "Who are you going with?"

Serena shrugged. "No one."

"You're going home alone? Early?"

"It'll be last call soon and I have an early morning meeting."

"On a Saturday morning?" Samantha exclaimed. It was truly unheard of.

Serena grinned. "There's a first time for everything, you know." She leaned forward and brushed a kiss across her sister's cheek, murmuring in her ear, "Have fun, but don't do anything I wouldn't do."

"That leaves an awful lot of wiggle room," Samantha said dryly.

"I know. Isn't it wonderful?" And with that, Serena sauntered out of the room.

"I wonder where Neil went," Jack said.

"Oh, I'm sure he's in the lobby, waiting for my sister. There's no way she's going home alone. You realize that, right?"

Jack let out a bark of laughter. "Good point." He spun Samantha around, settled his hands on her hips and kissed her gently. "And what about us, Samantha darling? Are *we* going home alone or—" He drawled out the final word suggestively.

The question took Samantha's breath away.

She knew exactly the answer she wanted to give him.

She wanted Jack like she'd never wanted a man before.

She shouldn't.

It wasn't wise to get involved with someone she worked with.

In fact, it would be rather reckless.

It was also the perfect moment to indulge her desires. After all, if she was doomed to recklessness anyway, why not indulge in an act she would thoroughly enjoy?

She leaned up and whispered in his ear, "Now why would I want to end my night all alone when you've spent the entire evening working me into a wickedly heated frenzy?"

Jack gave her that sexy grin of his and she about went up in flames.

Just to keep him on his toes, she said, "I mean, I guess there's Dick, but—"

"Dick? Who the hell is Dick?"

She grinned. "My vibrator."

"You named your vibrator?" Jack had an incredulous look on his face.

Samantha giggled. "Maybe."

"Well, no offense to *Dick*, but I'm pretty sure we can do better than whatever he's been providing."

Heat rushed through Samantha. "Promises, promises."

Chapter Six

SAMANTHA WOKE TO a pounding on her front door the next morning.

"What?" She lifted her head from where it was buried in her pillow and froze.

Sprawled at her side, sound asleep, was a gorgeous, naked Jack Saunders.

A barrage of memories exploded in her brain, all of them involving Jack and his annoying—delicious—grin, luscious body and very talented, very *wicked* tongue.

Dear goddess of chaos, she'd slept with Jack Saunders.

Before she could really even process what that meant, the pounding that had woken her began again.

"Huh?" Jack bolted upright. "What?"

Samantha sighed and climbed from the bed. "Just stay here. I'll deal with whoever it is." She grabbed her robe and struggled into it as she hurried out of the room and raced down the stairs to the front door.

One crisis at a time.

She'd send whoever was at the door on their way, then would figure out exactly what to say to get Jack out of her apartment so that she could fall apart in peace.

She flung open the door, but before she could say anything, Serena was pushing herself inside.

"You have to help me reverse the spells, Samantha. Our mother has lost her damned mind."

Samantha rolled her eyes, closed the door and followed her sister into the kitchen. It was too damn early in the morning for this.

"Why don't you have coffee made?" Serena demanded. "It's eleven o'clock. You should be on your second pot by now."

Samantha stared in horror at the clock on the microwave.

Unbelievable.

She'd overslept in a massive way, something she never did. Sleeping in on the weekends for Samantha meant getting up at six instead of five.

Now that she thought about it, though, she was pretty sure dawn had just been breaking when she and Jack had finally fallen asleep.

She shivered at her memories of the night before and stumbled to the kitchen table. Sinking into a chair, she watched as Serena started a pot of coffee.

That was going to take entirely too long. She needed to use the Keurig instead.

Serena let out a huff and spun around, hands on hips. "This is going to take entirely too long."

Samantha grinned.

It may drive their mother crazy, but their "twin-speak" as she called it was one of the best things about being twins. They couldn't hear each other's thoughts or anything, but somehow they tended to share them an awful lot, which could be quite beneficial in the right circumstances.

Too bad it wasn't fully functioning that morning. Either that or Samantha was simply too tired to anticipate what would happen next. She was expecting Serena to turn to the Keurig for some instant caffeine.

Instead though, Serena attempted to cast the coffeemaker, undoubtedly trying to make it produce coffee at a faster rate.

"No!" Samantha lunged to her feet, but it was too late.

The coffeemaker exploded and coffee spewed everywhere. And not just the tiny amount the coffeemaker had managed to produce thus far.

Oh no.

Serena's casting may have exploded the coffeemaker, but it also succeeded in making more coffee. It poured from the remnants of the coffeemaker, sliding over the counter and rushing over the side.

Without missing a beat, Serena grabbed two coffee cups and held them beneath the waterfall, filling them both. She passed one to Samantha, who scowled down into the black liquid.

"Seriously, Serena? It's probably full of glass!"

"Don't be ridiculous. Live a little, why don't ya?"

"Yeah, right before I die from ingesting glass."

Serena shrugged and raised the coffee cup to her lips.

Samantha lunged, grabbed it from her hands and rushed to the sink, where she dumped both cups.

"Oh, come on, Samantha. Where's that recklessness now?"

Samantha rolled her eyes, grabbed a K-cup and made them both a fresh cup of shard-free java. While the Keurig was doing its thing, Samantha dumped the remains of the coffeemaker into the trash, then wiped down the counter and the front of the cabinets.

She passed the first cup of coffee to Serena and got her own cup started. She then went back to the counter where her coffeemaker had once stood, flung open the cabinet above it and extracted her back-up.

"You have *two* coffeemakers?" Serena exclaimed incredulously. "*Plus* a Keurig?"

"I can't believe you're asking me that question," Samantha said as she plugged in the coffeemaker and set about making a new pot of coffee. "How many times have I told you, Serena, you can never be too prepared. In point of fact, I have *three* coffeemakers. This one is my back-up in case the first one breaks. The back-up for this one is still in its box in the pantry.

"Why on earth does your back-up need a back-up?"

"Are you kidding me right now? What if the back-up has a defect and suddenly there I am, with a broken coffee pot and a defective one, and no caffeine!"

"You'd still have your Keurig."

"Which could also go on the blink. Who knows? That's why I have a back-up for it as well."

"You're ridiculous. You know that right?"

"*I'm* ridiculous?" Samantha whirled and scowled at Samantha. "You're the one who caused a coffee waterfall in my kitchen."

"Touché. Very well, then. We're *both* ridiculous."

Samantha snorted. "Well, at least *my* ridiculousness will keep us supplied in caffeine for as long as we need it, unlike yours, which would have deprived us of it."

Serena grinned. "Touché again."

With the coffee pot slowly filling behind her, Samantha headed back to the Keurig, grabbed her cup and took a hefty gulp.

Ah. The nectar of the goddesses.

She closed her eyes and took another gulp, savoring the taste and smell. With a sigh, she set the cup aside. "Time for the drawer."

"What are you talking about?" Serena looked up. "What drawer?"

"The drawer your coffee waterfall poured over, and most likely *into*." Samantha strode back across the kitchen, opened the drawer and scowled inside. For a brief moment, she was seriously tempted to cast the drawer, rather than try to clean it out by hand.

"Come on, Samantha. Just cast the room clean, for heaven's sake!" Serena exclaimed.

"Right. Great idea." Samantha grabbed the container of silverware inside and tossed it into the sink. "Because I really want to explode more things in this room like you did, especially this drawer which happens to be full of *knives*."

"Mother will be so disappointed to know that her spell isn't working quite the way she intended."

Samantha rolled her eyes, but then decided she hadn't consumed anywhere *near* enough coffee for this task. She went back to her mug, intending to simply take one more big gulp before getting back to work, but once she had that gulp—so delicious—she realized she'd almost consumed the entire cup.

Might as well finish it while another one was brewing.

She set the Keurig to going again and eyed her sister while waiting for the giver of life to finish its job.

Serena was completely focused on her own cup of coffee, clearly not bothered even a little that her sister was stuck cleaning up the mess she had made.

Time to figure out what had her sister so unhappy.

Samantha headed for the table, mug in hand, only to realize Serena was staring into an empty mug herself. With a huff of exasperation, Samantha slid her cup toward Samantha, scooped up Samantha's and headed back to the Keurig.

At this rate, her sister would be here all day.

Samantha stiffened. And *Jack* was upstairs. This was *not* good. She needed to find out what was up with Serena and usher her out. The last thing Samantha needed was Serena discovering Jack's presence here.

She'd never hear the end of it!

Chapter Seven

"SO LET'S HAVE it." Samantha sat across from her sister, determined to speed things along. "What's the problem?"

"The spell," Serena spat. "Do you have any idea the havoc it's already wreaking on my life?"

Well, if it was anything close to Samantha's own experiences, she figured they were both doomed. Instead of admitting it though, she simply shook her head and took another gulp of coffee.

"First, I was bored yesterday. Bored! Then, I arrived at the event early and even helped you get set up. What's up with that? And then, to make matters worse, I actually worked this morning. On a Saturday!"

Samantha smirked. "Don't be absurd, Serena. You may fool others, even our mother with your lackadaisical attitude, but not me. I know how hard you work."

"Sh. That's our secret. Besides. I don't do weekends, not at the office anyway."

Samantha rolled her eyes. "Whatever. So you went into the office on the weekend. For once. That's not exactly going to destroy your life."

"No, but not having sex will!"

"What?" Samantha couldn't even imagine it. There was absolutely no way Serena was abstaining.

"You heard me. Last night I flirted with every unattached man at the event, but when it came time to seal the deal, nothing. All those marvelous tingles just disappeared as my brain began to misfire. I kept thinking   completely ridiculous things about how this man was probably a serial killer and that man was a total player. I mean who cares? I like players. I *am* one. And then *Neil!*"

"What about him? Don't tell me he finally made a move."

"Fine. I won't tell you that last night of all nights, he actually asked me to dance with him. Something he's never done before, mind you, and my goddess, that man is hot."

Eh. Samantha knew everyone found him charming and sexy, which okay, he was, but he didn't hold a candle to Jack.

Just the thought of Jack sent a rush of heat through her body as visions of their night together raced through her mind.

"Are you even listening to me?"

"Um, of course. I don't see what the problem is, though. I mean, you've wanted Neil for years."

"Exactly! Years spent fantasizing about that man and let me tell you, those fantasies have nothing against the reality of his *everything.*"

"Again. Not seeing the problem."

"The *problem* was my brain. While we were dancing and my body was going up in flames, my head was totally interfering with all the possibilities of the moment. All I kept thinking was he's kind of a jerk and he's probably just using me. Then I started wondering why he was acting all interested *now*. Right at the moment when I wasn't acting like myself, but instead was a walking, talking *Samantha* clone."

"Okay, one night without sex does not make you me, Serena."

"No, you're right. I'd need a decade for that, *at least.*"

Well. Maybe not a decade. But pretty close. "So, you didn't have sex with Neil then?"

"Of course not! I got to thinking how maybe he wanted you instead."

"Oh, that's ridiculous. Neil's never even looked at me that way. I've told you for years, when you're not watching, his eyes are tracking you everywhere. All you ever had to do was show a modicum of interest and he'd be all over you."

"Just like you and Jack?"

Samantha blushed. "No. Not at all like me and Jack. He hates me." Or at least he did. After last night, she wasn't quite sure about that anymore.

"Right. If only we were all so lucky as to have a guy hate us the way Jack does you," Serena said dryly. "Anyway, the point is, I couldn't turn off my brain. I was obsessing over every little thing, even as my body was going up in flames from Neil's delicious kisses. So in the end, I went home alone. From the pick-up event of the year. Who does that, Samantha? I mean, okay, you. But I'm not the good twin! That's your role. I'm supposed to have a different man in my bed every night and instead, last night, all I kept thinking about was how I didn't want a player. I was actually thinking in terms of a relationship. A *relationship,* Samantha. Then, to add insult injury, I actually had to take care of business *myself* last night." The look on Serena's face said it all. This truly was her worst nightmare.

"Um. Sorry?" Samantha really didn't know what to say. Before Jack, it'd been, what? Seven years since her last bit of naked fun. And really, now that she'd experienced a night with Jack, she was realizing she'd never really had naked fun at all before him. She'd just been checking boxes, as if having sex was a chore she had to complete. She'd given up that chore quite a while back, so she couldn't understand Serena's horror.

Although, after her night with Jack, maybe she could. After all, if what she'd had last night was what Serena was missing right now, perhaps she did understand after all.

Samantha was quite afraid that naked fun with Jack could become quite the addiction.

"Samantha! You're not even listening. What am I going to do? You have to help me."

"Isn't it a little early in the morning for crisis intervention?" A deep voice rumbled from the kitchen door.

Samantha froze.

Serena froze.

They stared at each other, Samantha in horror, Serena with a look of astonishment, then turned as one to glare at Jack, who stood in the doorway in all his delicious, wicked sexiness, barefoot, in jeans and nothing else.

For one moment, the kitchen was silent as the twins absorbed everything that was Jack Saunders in the morning, then they both exclaimed at the same time, "Seriously?"

"I told you to stay upstairs," Samantha said.

At the exact same moment, Serena exclaimed, "I went to bed all alone while the two of you were knocking boots all night long? I cannot believe it!" She whirled and stared at Samantha. "Is that why you overslept, you hussy?" The look on Serena's face was pure glee. "You slept with Jack Saunders!"

Samantha huffed in exasperation. "Yes, yes. And Jack was just leaving."

Jack grinned. "Coffee anyone?" As if it was his home and not hers, he headed straight for the coffeemaker, which had finally finished brewing its pot.

He paused when he saw the remnants of coffee and coffee grounds in the drawer, sink and on the floor, then turned and raised an eyebrow at Samantha.

She knew without him even saying a word that he wanted to know why she hadn't already cleaned it up with her magic. She could tell the moment he decided not to ask and instead chose to simply cast the room himself.

His magic stroked along her nerve endings, making her shiver with desire. She imagined she could hear it whispering promises of sexual delight as it swept by.

"Samantha?"

She shuddered and opened her eyes.

"Are you okay?" Serena was peering at her from across the table in concern. She didn't seem to have been affected at all by Jack's magic.

"Yes, of course, I'm fine. Just tired."

"I'm guessing you'd like a top-off then." Jack carried the coffee pot to her, but then hesitated. "Unless you used the Keurig?"

"Oh, we both used the Keurig," Serena said. "But don't worry.

Samantha carefully selects all her coffee products to ensure they will taste amazing even when mixed."

"Of course she does," Jack rumbled, then topped off both twins' mugs.

Samantha rolled her eyes. "You say that like it's a bad thing. Organization is the key to a happy life."

"I thought that was caffeine," Serena said.

"Fine. Organization and caffeine are the keys to a happy life."

Jack let out a deep chuckle. "And here I thought it was phenomenal sex."

Samantha groaned.

"Exactly!" Serena crowed.

Ugh. It really was too early to deal with both Jack *and* her sister.

"So what's the problem that brings you here so early in the morning, Serena?" Jack settled in a third chair at the table, a mug of coffee in his hands.

"First of all, it's not early," Samantha said, hoping to head Serena off at the pass. The last thing she needed was Jack's advice on their little dilemma. He'd probably advise her to enjoy the ride.

"Well, it's early for me," Serena groaned. "And while the curse may be working for you, Samantha, I cannot live this way!"

"Are you serious right now? You think this is working for me? I'm usually up by six on Saturdays."

"Dear goddess, why?" Jack rumbled.

"By now, I've usually done several hours of work, gone for a run —"

"I have to agree with Jack on that one. *Why on earth?*"

"—done a bit of gardening or cleaning, and should be on my way to the grocery store by now."

"All that before lunchtime?" Jack demanded.

"You see why our mother felt compelled to act," Serena said. "She needs help. She's all work and no play."

Jack grinned. "She got to play last night."

Samantha groaned. Great. These two were totally going to gang up on her. She could see it now. She'd let down her guard and now that they knew it was possible, they would never let her live it down *or* stop trying to convince her to do it again. She was doomed.

Serena giggled. "Good for you, Samantha. I mean, I guess the spell's not too bad a thing, then, right? If it means you're letting go of the good-twin persona, I suppose I can handle a couple weeks, just to make sure you get to live a little."

Samantha grimaced. "Don't do me any favors. Please."

"Hold on a minute." Jack raised his hand in the universal stop signal. "You mentioned something about this last night, Serena, and I never quite got the details. Explain, please."

"Didn't you wonder at all why Samantha's been acting so out of character? I mean, if you think she usually takes men home from our fundraising events, you're quite mistaken."

"Serena," Samantha groaned.

"Basically, our mother cast a spell of recklessness her way and apparently abstinence mine."

"Abstinence?" Jack let out a bark of laughter. "Your mother seriously cast an abstinence spell?"

"Of course she didn't. Serena's just being overly dramatic, as usual."

"Well, I'd like to see you survive without sex," Serena snapped, then grinned. "Oh, never mind, until our mother tossed recklessness your way, you probably had no idea what sexual desire was."

Jack grinned. "Well, if we have your mother's spell to thank for last night, I'd say job well-done."

Samantha rolled her eyes. Of course, he'd think that.

Serena huffed. "Normally, based on my own lackluster evening, I would disagree, but for you, sister, I'll make the supreme sacrifice." She stood. "I'll let you two get back to your canoodling."

Samantha stood quickly. "I'll walk you and Jack out."

Jack snorted, but made no move to leave the kitchen.

Serena giggled, hooked an arm in Samantha's and dragged her out of the kitchen and down the hall toward the front door. "He is *delicious*, Samantha. I am so jealous! I seriously want to go jump Neil's bones right now except—" She jerked Samantha to a stop, tilted her head and stared off into space.

"Except what?"

Serena made a sound of disgust and shook her head. "Except I'm thinking I should rope him into helping at the center instead."

Samantha's eyes widened. "Seriously? You're going to wrangle Neil so you guys can… work together?"

"I know!" Serena wailed. "It's terrible, I tell you. Just terrible!" She hurried to the door, flung it open and raced down the front steps. At the base of the stairs, she whirled and exclaimed, "The things I do for you, sister. You'd better appreciate it!"

Before Samantha could inform her that no, she didn't appreciate it at all and they needed to figure out how to counter their mother's castings, Serena had turned and raced down the sidewalk to where her car was parked in the driveway.

"Don't do anything I wouldn't," she called over her shoulder.

Samantha rolled her eyes. "That leaves an awful lot of room for a plethora of very dirty things." She blanched. Dear goddess. She couldn't *believe* she'd said that out loud.

Serena grinned. "Exactly!" She jumped into her car and peeled out.

Or at least that's what Samantha expected to happen.

Instead, she about fell over when Serena very carefully backed out of the driveway and sedately drove away, without even a single squeal of her tires.

"Are you sure you two didn't switch bodies or something?"

Samantha jumped in surprise, then whirled to confront Jack. "Are you seriously asking me if you slept with my sister last night?" She set her hands on her hips and glared at him.

Jack grinned. "Trust me. I know *exactly* who I slept with last night. The woman who has been driving me crazy with lust from the moment we met." With that, he swept her into his arms, kissed her breathless and then carried her back into her townhome, kicking the door shut behind them.

Chapter Eight

SAMANTHA WAS STILL thinking about that kiss and the way he'd carried her all the way to the bedroom without even a hitch in his stride and the deliciously wondrous hours that had followed as she drove to work Monday morning.

Yes.

Monday morning.

She and Jack had spent all of Saturday and Sunday in bed. Every time she'd mentioned she needed to do laundry or clean or garden or get to the grocery store, he'd distracted her with a kiss, in all kinds of delicious places, and she'd forgotten all about the many things on her to-do list.

They'd left the bedroom only for food and bathroom breaks and to grab more bottles of water. So much water, they'd eventually had to resort to drinking from the tap by the end of the weekend.

She, Samantha Covington, drinking *tap* water.

Okay, so there was a filter on the faucet, and yes, she knew that plastic was destroying the planet, but convenience and necessity sometimes meant making sacrifices, even though her mother glared and Serena most adamantly disapproved.

Jack, thankfully, hadn't said a word. He'd just gratefully accepted every water bottle she'd passed him and drank it down before turning his attentions back her way.

Now she was headed to work, having just kicked Jack out barely an hour before. He'd insisted they should shower together, which of course, had made her late. Again.

He'd also wanted them to go into the office together. She'd adamantly refused, of course. She shuddered to imagine it. He would have shown up to work in the same outfit he'd worn on Friday!

Okay, so probably no one would have noticed. Men were so spoiled that way.

But still.

Everyone would have noticed if they'd shown up in the same car.

And so she'd kicked him out.

He'd given her that sexy grin and said in his rumbly, growly voice, "I'll see you at the office, then."

Not if she could help it!

They headed up entirely different departments. There was no reason for him to visit her. Well, unless they needed to discuss one of their joint projects, but no. She'd simply tell Meredith to head him off at the pass. She'd lay down the law. Jack Saunders was not allowed in her office today.

This week.

No! This month. Yes. A month should do it.

A month of not seeing him and things would get back to normal. Surely her mother's spell would have worn off by then.

She had everything laid out in her mind, exactly what she was going to say to Meredith when she arrived at the office.

It would have worked too!

If only Jack hadn't beaten her there.

How did he *do* that?

Samantha stood in the doorway to her office and glared at Jack, who was sprawled in one of the leather chairs in her office, clearly waiting for her arrival. She opened her mouth to lambast him and he raised an eyebrow and grinned at her. Damn.

She stepped into the office and shut the door. "What are you doing in here?" she hissed at him. "I have work to do and I'm sure you do too."

"Yep."

Yep? Was that all he was going to say? Samantha stormed closer to him and glared down at him, hands on her hips. "So go do your work somewhere else that isn't here!"

Jack grinned up at her, stretched out his arms, then in one quick move, snagged her around the waist and toppled her into his lap.

Samantha let out a soft screech that he swallowed by planting his mouth on hers.

She clutched at his shoulders, opened her mouth to rant at him and he swept his tongue inside.

Heat raced through her and she lost herself in his kiss.

Long moments later, he pulled away with a gentle nip at her lips and a soft, murmured, "Good morning."

"Good morning," she whispered back.

Wait. What?

She shook her head and pulled away. "We already *said* good morning, plus goodbye to boot!"

Jack chuckled. "Ah, but not here at work, you see. I got to the office, but all I could think about was you down the hall and I knew I'd never make it through the day if I didn't get at least one more kiss to start us off right."

Samantha really wanted to roll her eyes, but her body clearly had other ideas. She melted into Jack and kissed him softly. "Good morning," she murmured again. "But you have to go away now, Jack. I have a meeting in—" She shook her head. "I don't even know when. Soon!" How could she not know what time it was? She always knew. She always—

"All right, then. No panicking." And in one move, in a massive show of strength that left Samantha gaping in awe, he surged to his feet, still holding her in his arms.

He let her legs go and lowered her gently to the ground, all the while kissing her breathless. "Have a good day, sweetheart." He walked to the door, opened it and headed out, tossing over his shoulder, "See you at lunchtime."

Samantha was almost to her desk when she realized what he'd said and whirled around.

He'd already disappeared though.

She shook her head, pushed Jack from her mind and got to work.

Despite Samantha's hysterical demand the Friday before, Meredith had apparently chosen not to cancel anything, for Samantha's morning was quite busy with several in-person meetings, a number of phone calls and a web conference.

When the web conference ended, she glanced at her calendar and realized she had nothing scheduled for a couple hours. That couldn't be right. Could it?

Unless Meredith had cancelled some things after all.

She reached for her phone to buzz Meredith when a knock on the jamb brought her head up.

"Lunch is here," Meredith said. "Enjoy!"

"Lunch? But I didn't—" Samantha broke off as Jack walked into her office with a number of bags from a local restaurant.

"Thanks, Meredith." He closed the door after her and started unpacking everything onto her work table. "I hope you're hungry, Samantha."

"I—" Samantha shook her head. "I'm sure I have a meeting scheduled or—"

"Actually, you don't. And I asked Meredith to guard the next hour for me. I told her we had a lot of work to do."

"But we don't. I mean, I *do*, but not with you. So—"

"We do have work to do. It's called eating." He grinned at her. "I brought your favorites and I'm counting on you to provide one of mine." He waggled his brows suggestively at her.

A wave of heat rushed through Samantha and she just knew she was blushing. Again! How did he do this to her every time?

She opened her mouth to argue with him, but then she caught a whiff of the food he had brought. "Enchiladas?"

"And queso and guacamole, plus sopapillas for dessert."

Well. She guessed it wouldn't be too bad of a thing to take a break. After all, she'd probably be more efficient with some food in her system.

Later, entirely too full from the incredible meal Jack had provided and almost giddy from the company, she realized taking a break had probably ruined her for the rest of the day, especially when Jack insisted on claiming numerous, steamy kisses on his way out the door.

They had talked and laughed through their lunch break, which had stretched from one hour to two. She perhaps wouldn't have even noticed the passage of time if Meredith hadn't discreetly knocked on the door to remind her that she had a meeting at two o'clock.

Two o'clock!

She, the master at time management, who was never late for anything, had somehow spent two hours in the middle of her work day doing nothing.

Nothing but flirting with Jack Saunders, that is.

Dear goddess, that man was devastating to her senses and at this rate, she had a feeling she'd be ruined as a businesswoman before the week was out.

The thought was so distracting, her three o'clock meeting was a disaster. Or maybe it was just short. She demanded everyone cut to the chase with their reports and had the meeting wrapped in twenty minutes.

Everyone looked a little stunned as they left the conference room, but Samantha couldn't be bothered to care.

She had other things to worry about.

"I'll be in my mother's office," she said to Meredith, then headed to the other end of the building to confront the woman who was making her life miserable.

Or wonderful.

She really wasn't sure.

But either way, it had to stop!

"Really, Mother, this has gone far enough." Samantha began speaking almost before she'd cleared the doorway. "You must end this casting at once. My life has to get back to normal before I go mad."

"Normal?" Serena popped her head up over the top of the chair where she'd apparently been slouching. "Are you seriously claiming that your life has been normal to date?"

Okay, that was a good point. "Well, normal for a witch anyway."

At that, their mother raised an eyebrow.

Samantha let out a huff. "Fine. Normal for *me* then, which is the way I like it, thank you very much."

"What did you have for breakfast this morning?" Serena asked.

"What?" Samantha shook her head. What did that have to do with anything?

"Well, come on, what did you have?"

"Nothing. I didn't have time for breakfast, which is exactly my point. My entire morning routine was disrupted and I was almost late for work!"

Serena smirked. "And I suppose you'd like us to believe that *disruption* wasn't anywhere near as *delicious* as your typical breakfast."

"Serena!" Their mother gasped.

"I'm just saying." Serena shrugged and grinned at Samantha. "So come on, admit it. There's no way you can honestly stand there and tell us you'd have preferred to have your spinach smoothie with a slice of plain toast, rather than Jack Saunders for breakfast this morning."

Samantha shivered at the memory of waking to Jack's exquisite attentions. She let out a huge sigh, only to come back to herself when Serena burst into laughter.

"What?"

"Nothing. You should just see yourself. Well, come on, sit down. Tell us how it was."

Samantha drew back in horror. Had Serena seriously just asked her to share with her and *their mother* how delicious Jack Saunders was in bed?

"Serena, you know better," Elizabeth admonished. "For heaven's sake, your sister didn't even tell me when she started her period. I found out years later when I was worried and wanted to take her to the doctor because she hadn't yet started."

Samantha stared at her mother in horror. "Are you seriously talking about this right now?" She shook her head. "I can't even—" What had she even come in for? Certainly not to talk about such intimate subjects as menstruation and Jack's brand of sexy.

Dear goddess, she'd forgotten completely why she was there. What if it was important? What if it was for a client? What if—

Serena snickered. "I remember that. It took me forever to figure out that she was stealing my tampons. All because she was too embarrassed to mention she needed her own supply."

"Would you just stop it?" Samantha shrieked. "Stop talking about menstruation!"

The sound of a throat clearing made her freeze.

No.

She absolutely refused to turn around because it wasn't Jack. He wasn't standing in the doorway listening to her shriek like a shrew about her menstruation cycle.

Dear goddess.

Anyone but Jack.

She slowly turned on her heel and closed her eyes at the sight of Jack standing in her mother's doorway, a giant grin on his face.

"I can come back, Elizabeth, if this isn't a good time."

"No, no. Come in, Jack. My daughters were just leaving."

Serena stood, hooked her arm in Samantha's and dragged her past Jack. "We'll see you later, Jack."

Long moments later, Samantha collapsed on the couch inside her office and stared at the ceiling. Maybe she should move.

To China.

Or maybe Mars.

Mars would be good.

Serena giggled and shoved a water bottle into Samantha's hand. "Don't be ridiculous, Samantha. What on earth would you do on Mars?"

"What happened?" Meredith asked, hovering in the doorway.

Samantha should probably tell her she was fine, but really, she wasn't. She wasn't fine at all.

She'd been shrieking.

Shrieking.

In her mother's office.

About menstruating.

Why had they even been talking about such a ridiculous subject?

Surely it wasn't her fault.

Was it?

"I've lost it," Samantha groaned.

"She lost it?" Meredith repeated.

"A tiny bit, yeah," Serena said. "Of course, since it's Samantha, it was kind of the equivalent of a full-fledged breakdown."

"I *shrieked* at you," Samantha whispered.

"What was she shrieking about?"

"Menstruation."

Samantha shuddered. She most definitely, couldn't possibly have been the one to bring that up, right? She would *never*.

"I've never known Samantha to mention that time of month at all," Meredith observed.

"Oh, she definitely doesn't. If she hadn't stolen my tampons when we were teens, I'd swear she never menstruated at all."

"Yeah, that sounds about right," Meredith agreed.

Samantha surged up from the couch, shrieking, "Why are you *still* talking about menstruating?" She then collapsed back down and stared at the ceiling.

Dear goddess, she really had lost it.

She would never have even *mentioned* that word anywhere, let alone at work, before her mother's casting.

"This is all Mother's fault."

"Well, yeah, I have to agree with that," Serena said. "But look on the bright side. You got to shake the sheets with Jack Saunders."

"What?" Meredith, who had turned to leave the office, swung back around and stared at Samantha. "Is that true?"

Samantha just waved a hand in the air. "I mean. A little bit, yeah."

"A little bit," Serena snorted. "That's kind of like saying you're a little bit pregnant. I guarantee there's no way a man as sexy as Jack Saunders was only banging the headboard *a little bit.*"

Samantha lifted her head just enough to glare at her sister. "Would you stop it with the euphemisms? We had sex. That's all."

Serena let out a hoot of laughter. "Oh, well, then. I'm sorry. You had *sex* all weekend long."

"All weekend long!" Meredith gasped. "Is that true?"

Samantha turned her head and glared at them. "You know what? I could fire you both."

"I'm family. You can't fire your family," Samantha said.

"And you'd be lost without me," Meredith said.

Samantha nodded. "It's true. But I'd be willing to risk it, I think."

"You'd be late for every meeting," Meredith predicted. "Your notes would be a mess and you'd never be able to find the right document at the right time."

Samantha groaned. "Fine. You're not fired."

Meredith grinned. "Now tell us *everything*."

"He's making me crazy!" Samantha surged to a sitting position and swung around to face her sister and assistant. "What am I supposed to do? I can't have him coming in here, distracting me from my day with his good morning kisses and flirty lunches and—"

"Wait a minute," Serena said. "You guys have been bumping uglies *at work?*"

Samantha blanched. "Of course not! We would *never!*"

Meredith grinned. "But Jack did beat her into the office this morning and then he brought her lunch. I thought you guys were just working on a project or something, but now I realize. He's courting you, isn't he?"

"Aww, that's so sweet!" Serena exclaimed.

Samantha was horrified. "What? No! How could you say that? He's just—just torturing me, that's all! Making me laugh and kissing me and bringing me lunch and distracting me from my work and—and—"

"It's called courting, Samantha," Serena said dryly.

"Exactly," Meredith agreed.

Chapter Nine

IT WAS PROBABLY the cowardly thing to do, but after Meredith and Serena convinced Samantha that Jack wasn't just messing with her, Samantha sneaked out of the office.

Early.

She usually stayed until around seven o'clock on Mondays, but she decided to hell with it. The paperwork would still be there in the morning.

Actually, now that she thought about it, that decision was kind of disturbing as well. She'd actually packed everything into her briefcase, intending to work from home, but then she'd just stood there in her office, staring at her briefcase for long moments before eventually deciding to leave it all behind.

She couldn't *believe* she'd left her work at *work*.

This was getting a little out of hand, but somehow she couldn't even find it in herself to care.

All the way down the elevator, she told herself when she reached the ground floor, she'd let everyone else off, but then would turn right back around and get back on it. She'd go up to the ninth floor, grab her briefcase and take all that work home with her.

In fact, once she was back in her office, maybe she'd unpack that work and just do her job.

At work.

The way she did every Monday.

But then they reached the lobby and she left the elevator with everyone else. She walked past the guard, waving goodbye to him as she walked straight out the front door. She headed to the parking lot and the entire way she told herself she was being irresponsible.

Only to find that *she just didn't care.*

She reached her car, opened the door and slung her purse onto the passenger seat. She was about to climb in when she heard it.

A tiny meow.

She froze, one foot inside the car and looked around.

Surely that was just her imagination.

She started to lower into the seat and she heard it again.

Only this time, she heard several meows.

She let out a huff of exasperation.

Seriously?

All she wanted to do was go home.

But that tiny, plaintive meow.

She should just ignore it.

Mew, mew, mew.

Okay. Even she couldn't ignore that.

With a giant sigh, she climbed back out of the car, closed the door and began the search.

It took her twenty minutes.

Twenty minutes to find and capture the three kittens who were playing in a parking lot.

A parking lot!

"You three just aren't very smart. You know that, right?" She said to them as she settled them into a box she'd had in the trunk of her car. "Now stay there while I make sure I haven't missed any of your siblings. Or your mama for that matter."

Another thirty minutes to check down every row, under every car until finally she was convinced there were no more kittens running around, risking life and limb.

She climbed back into the car and stared into the box she'd placed on the passenger seat. The three kittens had all curled up together and were now sound asleep.

She tried not to notice how utterly adorable they were. One of the kittens was completely gray while the other two were pitch black.

"What am I going to do with you three?" She demanded. "I can't take you home with me. I don't have time to take care of cats. Believe me, you'd be better off with someone else."

But who. That was the question.

She pulled out her phone and did a search for animal control.

Except.

Was animal control no-kill? She didn't actually know.

Fine, then.

She'd call the Humane Society.

They would certainly take these babies in and find them a good home.

She found the information for the Humane Society, but then just hovered there a moment, hesitant to engage the call.

It wasn't like the kittens would be able to roam free at a shelter. They'd have to be put in a cage so that people could meet them and maybe adopt them, something she'd heard could take a while, especially for black cats.

How long would these babies be stuck in a cage?

And what if they were never adopted?

What if they ended up spending their entire lives locked up?

Samantha made a sound of exasperation.

Fine then.

She'd just take them home with her.

She had the room and it seemed like the right thing to do.

She wouldn't keep them, of course. That would be utterly irresponsible.

She'd just take care of them until she could find them a good home.

Of course, she'd need a few things at the house.

What did cats require anyway?

Another search on her phone and she had a list of everything she needed to keep three kittens happy and healthy.

"I hope you guys appreciate this," she told her tiny hitchhikers as she pulled out of her parking space. "I have a feeling you're going to be a rather expensive good deed."

As it turned out, they were not only expensive, but time-consuming, something Samantha discovered as she wandered the aisles of a pet store, trying to make decisions she'd never had to make before.

Who knew there were so many cat food options? Wet. Dry. Grains.

No grains. Everything in between. And cat treats. *So many* cat treats.

Not to mention everything else she had to buy.

Food and water bowls.

Litter boxes. (Apparently she needed four, which seemed rather excessive. Then again, her townhome had two and a half bathrooms and she lived alone so…)

Kitty toys.

Perches for the windows.

Cat beds because there was no way the fur balls were sleeping with her. What if she rolled over and squashed them in the middle of the night?

Cat scratchers.

What else?

She stared at her jam-packed cart.

She didn't exactly have room for the cat tree she'd been admiring.

Still, cats *should* have something to climb.

Maybe it would discourage them from destroying her drapes.

She pushed the cart to the front of the store, dragging the cat tree behind her.

Fifteen minutes and five hundred dollars later, her car trunk was full, but there was no way the cat tree was ever going to fit inside her BMW.

For a split second, she was tempted to use her magic to shrink the tree. With her luck, though, she'd end up shrinking her car and the kittens with it.

Jack had a truck though.

Before she could second-guess that thought, her phone was in her hand and she was texting Meredith.

Fifteen minutes later, Jack showed up in his black pickup, grinning at her from the drivers' seat.

Great. Talk about shooting herself in the foot.

How had she already forgotten the plan to avoid Jack for at least a month?

On the other hand, maybe he would take a kitten.

Better yet, maybe he'd take all three.

Oh, yes.

This plan had possibilities.

* * *

Jack's annoyance when he realized Samantha had sneaked out of the office, but hadn't yet shown up at her apartment, turned into triumph when Meredith called to tell him Samantha needed his help.

Something about his truck.

"The Pet Emporium?" He repeated incredulously.

"Don't ask me," Meredith said. "As far as I know, Samantha has no pets."

Jake had to agree. Unless they'd been hiding all weekend long, he knew she didn't have any. So he couldn't imagine what she was doing at the Pet Emporium that required his truck, but he wasn't one to look a gift horse in the mouth.

Fifteen minutes later, he realized he didn't know Samantha half as well as he thought he did.

"So you rescued them?"

"Well, someone had to do it!"

"You could have taken them into the offices. I bet someone there would have been thrilled to adopt them." Jack could tell by the look on Samantha's face that hadn't even occurred to her. "In fact, you could have taken them to the Humane Society."

"And seen them locked in a cage for who knows how long?" Samantha demanded.

Jack grinned. "Admit it. You fell in love with the kittens."

"They're not staying!"

Jack lifted an eyebrow and looked from her to the giant cat tree standing in the space between her car and his truck. It was the largest tree he'd ever seen. "They didn't have smaller ones?"

A blush crept into Samantha's cheeks. "It had to be big enough for all three of them."

Jack glanced into her car at the ridiculously tiny kittens who were scrambling all over the seats. "Yes, I can see how you thought nothing smaller would do."

Samantha glared at him. "They can grow into it!"

"You're right about that." Jack chuckled, then grabbed the cat tree and hefted it into the bed of his truck. "I'll follow you, princess." He sauntered around the truck, headed for the driver's side.

* * *

Samantha growled low in her throat. She hated it when he called her that!

A quick glance inside the car showed her one kitten sitting in the driver's seat while another was clinging to the headrest of the passenger seat. She didn't see the third kitten at first, which caused her a moment of panic, but then movement in the backseat caught her eye. The third kitten was currently climbing its way up the leather toward the back window well.

Normally the thought of kitten claws creating tiny puncture marks in the leather would be rather distressing.

For some reason, though, Samantha's heart melted at the sight of the kittens playing. Even wreaking havoc on her leather seats, they were absolutely adorable. This was all her mother's fault!

With a quick shake of the head, she carefully opened the drivers' side door, scooped up the kitten sitting there and slid in, shutting the door behind her.

She held the kitten up to her face, kissed it on its nose and said, "You need to be good for the ride home now, you hear?" She set the kitten into the box, extracted kitten number two from the headrest and settled it into the box with its sibling.

Samantha looked over her shoulder at the third kitten and decided he (she?) looked stable enough. The kitten had completed its climb and was now curled in the back window well, sound asleep.

She drove carefully back to her place, relieved to note that her mother's spell wasn't strong enough to impact her driving skills. If she ended up driving like her sister, with the speeding tickets to go with it, it would be the last straw!

She'd almost made it home when she realized she'd forgotten to con Jack into taking the kittens. Damn! She could have been following him to his house right now.

Maybe it wasn't too late. She'd just avoid unloading them before talking to Jack. As soon as they got to the house, she'd—

She froze, hands locked on the steering wheel, trying desperately not to squeal or jerk the wheel as tiny kitten paws kneaded her thigh through her skirt.

The final blocks to her townhome were incredibly stressful as Samantha battled to keep the three kittens from climbing down to her feet.

By the time she pulled into her driveway, she had one kitten perched on her shoulder, another curled up in her lap and a third, the most determined to reach her feet, cuddled to her chest with her right hand as she carefully steered with her left.

She breathed a loud sigh of relief as she pulled into her garage and put the car into park.

She sat there, not even daring to move as she listened to the sounds of tiny kitten purrs.

A knock on her window startled all four of them. The kitten in her lap sat up and let out a tiny hiss, making Samantha giggle. "It's okay, baby," she whispered as she pressed the button to lower the window.

Jake leaned over, one arm braced against the top of her car. "You planning on staying in the car all night?"

"I can't move," Samantha told him. In the time it had taken her to roll down the window, the kitten on her right shoulder had carefully stepped its way to her left and now sat there, batting at her earring.

Jack chuckled. "Here." He reached in and scooped the kitten from her shoulder, then accepted the one Samantha was holding.

Samantha picked up the third kitten, who seemed perfectly content to sit on her lap all night long, and after a quick kiss, passed that one to him too.

Jack stepped back and Samantha opened her door and stepped out. That was when she got a good look at Jack.

The man was sexy with a capital everything. But standing there, giant hands gently cradling three tiny kittens to his chest, he made Samantha's girly parts squeal.

It should be illegal.

"What should?" Jack rumbled.

Samantha waved a hand at him. "All of that."

He raised an eyebrow. "The kittens?"

"Them too."

He grinned. "Let's get them settled, shall we?" With that, he turned and headed for the door that led from the garage into Samantha's home.

Jack had disappeared inside before she managed to pull herself together and race after him. By the time she got inside, he had let the kittens loose in the living room where the three were exploring everything.

Samantha stood, hands on hips, scowling at Jack.

"Oh, I'm sorry. Was there somewhere else you wanted them?"

"Yes. Your house," Samantha snapped.

Jack raised an eyebrow. "Don't you think it's a little soon for you to be moving in with me? Not that the suggestion doesn't have merit, but —"

Samantha gasped. "I am not suggesting anything of the sort!"

Jack chuckled, then reached out and snagged her around the waist, pulling her into his arms. "Of course not," he murmured against her lips, then wiped her thoughts away with a searing kiss.

Long drugging moments later, Jack lifted her in his arms and carried her up to her bedroom, where he had his wicked, *wicked* way with her.

Dear goddess of chaos, the man was potent!

Chapter Ten

AN ETERNITY LATER, Samantha lay sprawled across her king-sized bed, Jack at her side, both of them naked and breathing hard.

It took long moments for Samantha's brain to kick in, but when it did—"The kittens!" She bolted upright.

"Aw, they'll be fine."

"Are you kidding me right now?" She jumped out of bed and scrabbled around for her clothes.

Jack reached for her, but she darted away.

"Hands off!" She exclaimed. "I haven't set up anything for them. They don't have any food or water—and where is my bra?" She whirled and glared at Jake, who just grinned back at her.

Finding and rejecting her underwear, which was nothing more than a useless, shredded piece of lace at that point, she grabbed Jack's shirt where it lay on the floor and jerked it on instead. Not wanting to take the time to find alternate underwear, she was gratified to see the shirt fell to mid-thigh.

"Come back to bed, Sam." Jack's voice was deep and lust-filled, making Samantha shiver in delight.

"Not a chance. I have to get the kittens settled. I can't believe I let you distract me like that. They've probably destroyed everything and —" Her eyes widened in horror. "We didn't set up the litter boxes!" She bolted for the bedroom door, the sound of Jack's laughter following her as she raced down the hall toward the stairs. She couldn't believe she'd abandoned the poor darlings.

Reaching the top of the stairs and glancing over the rail, she froze.

The upper railing overlooked the open concept of her townhome, giving her a view of not just the hall, but the living room, dining room and kitchen.

The kittens had obviously gotten into the toilet paper stored in the half bath at the bottom of the stairs because there was a trail of tattered toilet paper pretty much everywhere. The trails led from the bathroom door into the living room, across the couch and under a chair, over the coffee table and around a lamp, into the kitchen and back out again, into the dining room, in and out and around the table legs.

Basically, the house looked like it had been teepeed by a bunch of drunken teenagers.

"Damn. How much toilet paper you figure that is?" Jack rumbled behind her.

Samantha shook her head. "All of it."

Jack laughed. "And how much is that?"

"Depends on if they got into the new pack or just grabbed the roll off the spool."

"There's no way that's just one roll," Jack said.

Samantha shrugged. "I buy the jumbo rolls. It's more efficient and cost effective."

"Of course you do."

"I'd better find the kittens, not to mention clean up this mess." Samantha headed down the stairs, Jack right behind her.

"You do that. I'll bring in the litter boxes and cat tree," Jack said.

Samantha found the kittens curled up in her basket of blankets in the living room. They'd obviously worn themselves out teepeeing the downstairs so Samantha got busy cleaning up their mischief. Along the way, she noted a bit of tattered leather on the bottom of her sofa and apparently one kitten had decided the fake ficus tree in the corner would serve as a litter box. That would be going straight to the curb.

"What on earth are you doing?"

Samantha jumped and glanced up from where she was trying to untangle a long piece of toilet paper wrapped around the legs of the dining room table.

Jack stood in the entry between the living and dining room, hands on hips, grinning at her.

"I'm cleaning up this mess, of course," Samantha told him as she struggled to lift the leg enough to extract a tiny piece of paper from beneath it. How on earth the paper had even gotten under there, she had no idea.

"Sure, but you're a witch. There're about a million easier ways to do that."

Samantha let out a huff of exasperation, sat back on her heels and glared at Jack. "This situation certainly does *not* call for magic."

Jack grinned. "Since I've never actually seen you casting any kind of spell at all, why don't you tell me the type of situation you believe *would* call for magic?"

"I don't know. Something life threatening or horribly dangerous. Saving a kid from drowning or—or—I don't know. Something big."

"And how often do you encounter drowning children?"

"Oh, whatever." Samantha turned back to the table, only to find it lifting off the ground and the paper she'd been struggling with winding free. The table settled back down and the paper zipped by Samantha, colliding mid-air with other streams of toilet paper moving toward it.

The kittens came awake and bounded across the room, chasing the surge of Jack's power, or perhaps the toilet paper swept up in its wake. The paper landed in a pile in the middle of the living room and the kittens pounced.   The paper flew up in every direction before responding to Jack's magic and returning to the same pile the kittens were busy demolishing.

The feel of Jack's power was masculine and potent, making Samantha shiver with desire, which just made her crankier. "That was entirely unnecessary. I had the situation under perfect control!" She surged to her feet and glared at him.

"Of course, you did. But as far as I can tell, Samantha, you're wasting your gifts. What's the point of being a witch if you never tap into your powers?"

"I prefer to be in perfect control, thank you very much."

Jack looked confused. "I know this. I just don't understand what that has to do with using your magic."

Samantha huffed. "Have you *seen* Serena's castings?"

Jack grinned. "Her castings *are* legendary."

"Exactly!"

"But you're not Serena."

"No. I'm not. And I'd like to stay that way. We're twins, Jack. Maybe not identical, but that doesn't matter when it comes to magic. We pull from the same well so when her castings go out of control, what do you suppose happens to my abilities?"

Jack frowned. "Okay, it's true twins have intertwined powers and abilities, but that doesn't mean they're not individuals and can't have individual control. They just have to work harder at it."

Samantha raised an eyebrow. "And what makes you think we didn't work at it? We took all the required courses in magic and I'm telling you, it was always an exercise in chaos."

"And did you continue practicing after college?"

"Of course not! I mean, what would be the point?"

"Because a young witch's magic is supposed to be a bit unstable. That's the reason for the courses. Witches don't gain full control until they reach their majority!"

"Well, I was tired of the chaos, so shoot me. I just wanted some control and once we graduated and were on our own, I finally got my chance!"

"Wait. So are you saying that you don't use your magic at all?"

"Not if I can help it."

"You just keep it all bottled up? How does it not explode all the time?"

Samantha shrugged. "It used to, but it got easier over time."

"Yeah. Because you're killing your gift."

"If that's the consequence for having an orderly life, I'll take it."

"An orderly life? Samantha, you might as well be human."

"I've got news for you, Jack. We're all human."

"You know what I mean."

"Look, it's not like I *never* use my magic." Even though she really didn't. "I'm just not very good at it and Serena's *too* good at it. Between the two of us, we're just malfunctioning witches and that's all there is to it. I decided long ago, it was best to only use my powers in emergency situations."

"But that's not the way it works! If you don't use your magic, it won't come to you when you *do* need it."

She shrugged. "Then it won't come to me. And that's fine. At least it won't be bouncing all over the place, causing havoc and chaos in my everyday life the way it does in Serena's."

"And when was the last time you used your magic? For real?"

There was absolutely no way on earth Samantha was sharing that story. It had taken her years to live it down and if by some miracle, Jack had never heard about it, she wasn't going to be the one to share it.

"Samantha?"

"It's been a while."

"How long's a while?"

A long while.

That dick Maurice had been harassing her at work. She'd been fresh out of college and determined to blend in and not be seen as one of the privileged Covingtons. As a result, she'd tolerated Maurice's misogynistic attitude and had avoided him as much as possible, but then one day, he'd cornered her in the break room, copped a feel and her magic had exploded out of control.

This, of course, had resulted in her mother getting involved, and when *she'd* found out exactly why Samantha's magic was raging around the office, she'd fired him on the spot and had security escort him out.

No one had ever tried to flirt with Samantha again.

At least not until Jack had joined the office three years later.

"Was it seriously that long ago?" Jack demanded.

Samantha shrugged.

"Oh, shit. Don't tell me that asshat made you stop using your magic!"

"Of course not. And how do you know about him?"

Jack arched an eyebrow. "Seriously? Every witch hired is told the story of you blowing a ten-block grid and destroying the company's electronics with it."

Samantha groaned. "Great."

"Hey, it's a fantastic story. I especially love the part where the asshat was sobbing hysterically from the punch your magic delivered to his groin."

"He deserved it." Samantha scowled.

Jack grinned. "And that right there is why the story is so effective."

"What are you talking about?"

"It lets all the asshats know that harassment of any kind will not be tolerated. But we've gotten off track. Tell me you've used your magic since then."

Samantha sighed. "I was already avoiding using my magic because it was so damn unpredictable. What happened with Maurice just reinforced my decision."

"So is that a no? As in you haven't used your magic since?"

"That's a no."

"But you hadn't even reached your majority yet, right?"

"I was close enough."

"How close?"

"I was twenty-three."

"So you still had two years to go."

"Eighteen months, but yes."

"So how do you know you can't control your magic if you haven't tried since reaching the age of majority?"

"Because Serena *has* tried."

"I keep telling you, Samantha. You're *not* Serena. Besides, I wouldn't be surprised if her magic is so chaotic because she's drawing from the same well yours has been bottled up in. Of course, her magic is wild and untamed! You've done nothing but contain yours in the same well hers tends to explode from."

It couldn't possibly be that easy.

"What could it possibly hurt for you to at least try? Just tap into your magic a tiny bit. Look. The kittens are making a mess again. Just use your magic to clean the room."

Samantha grit her teeth. She couldn't understand why everyone always reacted like this when she told them why she wouldn't use her magic. It wasn't as if there was a law that said all witches had to use their powers, now was there? Of course not! Yet somehow, no matter who they were, every witch seemed to take offense at her decision.

"Come on. Just try."

Fine. She would prove to him exactly what happened when she used her magic. He'd see firsthand the disaster and—

Wait. No.

That was her mother's spell speaking.

She would *not* be demonstrating anything.

It was entirely too risky.

Of course, it *would* be interesting to see what happened. She hadn't even attempted to use her magic in years.

But no.

She wasn't ready to risk turning her life upside down just because her mother had cast a spell.

Although Jack *was* right. In an emergency, she would probably be in quite the pickle. Over the years, she'd occasionally considered changing her mind, but she'd ultimately decided that an ordered, controlled everyday existence was well worth the potential loss of her magic in an emergency situation.

Tapping into her magic now after so many years of it lying dormant would probably be tantamount to setting off an earthquake.

It would be really fun to find out though.

No. Not fun. Reckless.

"Samantha?"

"It's too risky."

"To use your magic? It shouldn't be risky at all. It should be second nature!"

"Ugh. You sound just like my mother."

"Ah. I take it, this is why she cast that spell?"

Of course it was, which meant this was all her mother's fault. Because of her spell, Samantha was once again tempted to tap into the magic she'd smothered long ago.

"Samantha?"

"Maybe I could try. Or not. No. I don't know why I said that. This is a terrible idea."

"I think it's brilliant. And I'm here to help if need be."

Great. Just what she needed. Jack. The sexiest man she'd ever met. The man who sent her body up into flames on a regular basis, witnessing her inability to control her magic.

"Just try, Samantha."

She groaned. "Fine." She closed her eyes and went searching.

It took a few moments to even find the power.

The well that had once been so easily—*too* easily—accessible was now shadowed and dark, walled off.

Goddess of light, did she really want to risk tearing that wall down?

Her eyes flew open. "Jack, I'm not sure about this. You have no idea how hard it was to contain my powers. If I let them loose and I can't control them, I don't know that I'll be able to put the genie back in the bottle."

"Samantha, you were born a witch. You were born to wield whatever powers you possess. I'll be here to help you. Just, for once, let go of your infamous control. Just let the power *be.*"

"But—"

"I won't let anything bad happen, Samantha. I promise."

She looked at the kittens who were still bounding around the room, playing with toilet paper. "Maybe we should—"

"Just try, Samantha."

With a huff, she closed her eyes, took a deep breath and sank back down toward the well of her power. The wall was still there, standing strong.

She hesitated, then imagined her hands reaching through the wall, grabbing hold of the power lying dormant within and yanking it free.

Chapter Eleven

JACK WOKE TO the sensation of a scratchy tongue licking his ear and tiny claws kneading his chest. He opened his eyes to find he was stretched out on the ground with one kitten on his chest and another sprawled across his face.

"What happened?" He caught the face-kitty in one hand and struggled to sit up.

Samantha was sitting on the floor, back against the living room wall, the third kitten, the gray one, cradled in her hands.

"I could have hurt them," she said.

"What?"

"Your stupid idea. Letting my power just *be*. It could have killed us. I'm lucky it didn't take out the kittens."

"Don't be ridiculous. I don't know what happened, but—"

"My power exploded, that's what happened. It knocked you out and I haven't been able to contain it since. I told you this would happen!"

Jack caught the second kitten who'd been perched on his chest in his hand and struggled to his feet. He staggered over to where Samantha was sitting, set his back to the wall and slowly slid down to sit beside her. He settled the two kittens in his lap, nudged Samantha with his shoulder and said, "It can't possibly be that bad. I mean look at the place. Where'd all the toilet paper go?"

"Incinerated."

Jack raised an eyebrow. "Really? Where are the ashes?"

"They're gone too."

He studied the room again. "And the furniture?"

"I don't know. The power exploded, you went down like a tree in a storm, the toilet paper all went up in flames with no ashes left behind, and all the furniture just disappeared."

"Damn."

"I know, right? I'm afraid to check the rest of the house. I just made sure you were breathing and the kittens weren't harmed and that was enough for me."

"What were you thinking about when the power exploded?"

"You told me to concentrate on cleaning the room so I did."

Jack grinned. "Well, I'd say you did an excellent job."

"Are you crazy?"

"Check out the carpet. It looks brand new. Not a single stain or speck of dirt anywhere."

Samantha sighed. "I suppose."

"I'm also not seeing any dust on the walls or the built-in bookshelves, plus not a single streak on the mirror over the fireplace. I'd say your magic is working perfectly."

"It took away my furniture!"

"Okay, there are a few glitches, but overall, things could be much worse."

"I don't see how!"

"Well, considering the dining room table is still present, I'd say your magic was probably contained to just the living room, which means you can still watch TV in the bedroom."

* * *

Samantha rolled her eyes.

What a ridiculous, man thing to say.

As long as there was a TV somewhere, he was fine.

Well, Samantha happened to like her giant leather couch, thank you very much. And she would miss her coffee table. It was perfect for propping her feet up after a long day of work. She also wanted her side tables back. She needed them to hold her coffee and magazines.

At least the ficus plant was gone, though. That was one bonus.

Oh, shit.

"Jack?"

"Yes?"

"Were all the cat things in the living room?"

"Uh."

Samantha groaned.

"It's not as bad as you might think. I set up the litter boxes in the garage and most everything else I left in the entryway."

Well, thank goddess for small favors.

"So what *was* in the living room?"

"Not much. Just one thing."

"*What* one thing?"

Jack cleared his throat. "The cat tree."

"Are you kidding me? The most expensive item is the one thing my magic disappeared?"

Jack grinned. "Well, it could be worse."

"I don't see how!"

"We could be without any litter boxes."

This was true. That would be worse.

"I need to get the kittens set up." Samantha struggled to her feet and was halfway across the living room before she remembered the plan. She swung back around. "Unless you'd like to adopt them? They clearly adore you."

Jack grinned, glanced down at the two kittens in his lap, then up at Samantha. "Oh, I wouldn't think of stealing these darlings from you. Smoky in particular would be devastated." He nodded at the little gray kitten who had followed Samantha across the room and was now playing with the strap of her sandal.

"Smoky?"

He grinned. "Didn't think I heard you naming him, did you?"

"It was an adjective."

"Yes. Your smoky little darling, I heard. But I think that's the perfect name for him. Smoky."

She sighed. "Fine. What about the others?"

"Don't try and pretend you don't already have names in mind for them as well. Come on. Share with the class."

Samantha shrugged. "I was thinking maybe Midnight and Shadow."

"I like it. Smoky, Midnight and Shadow." Jack lifted Midnight and Shadow from his lap and set them on the floor, then surged to his feet and sauntered across the room to where Samantha was standing. When he reached her, he snaked an arm around around her waist and drew her close for a hot, demanding kiss. Long moments later, he pulled back to murmur, "Let's get these darlings set up, shall we?"

The hours passed quickly in Jack's presence. He made Samantha laugh, even when she didn't want to, even when they were dealing with the annoying after-effects of her magic, which included the discovery of her living room furniture on the front lawn, necessitating both muscle and magic to return everything where it belonged.

By the time they were finished, though, Samantha's living room looked more lived-in than it ever had. Her couch, coffee table, end tables and TV were all returned to their rightful spots, but interspersed throughout the room were cat toys and cat beds, scratchers and in the corner where the ficus tree had once stood, a giant cat tree had been moved in.

The kittens were in heaven, chasing balls all over the first floor and climbing all over the cat tree.

Jack had talked Samantha into ordering pizza for dinner and they were now stretched out on the living room couch, watching TV.

"How's the magic?" Jack asked.

Samantha was stretched out on top of him, her cheek resting against his chest and she could feel the vibration of every word.

"I'm not sure. It's good, I think."

"Want to try a new casting?"

Jack had been trying to get her to cast a new spell ever since the last one disappeared all her furniture, but she'd been too nervous to try. "Maybe tomorrow."

"I'm going to hold you to that."

She rolled her eyes. Of course, he would. She had no idea how he'd managed to somehow finagle his way into spending the entire evening with her, but he had and now she found herself completely content to just lie there and enjoy his company. Normally, she'd be doing some last minute paperwork for the company or chores around the house or paying bills or something equally productive.

After a terribly unproductive weekend, she'd followed it up with a fairly unproductive Monday.

This was unheard of.

And yet, she couldn't regret it.

Somehow—

"You're thinking so loudly," Jack rumbled. "Relax, Samantha."

She grinned. "I am relaxing, you doofus."

"Huh. Must be all that thinking going on that confused me." He curled up, pulling her up at the same time so that he could capture her lips with his.

Heat flashed through Samantha. Good goddess, the man could kiss!

* * *

Samantha was still recovering from Jack's kisses and everything that followed the next day at work.

Jack had stayed over again the night before and somehow the next morning, it hadn't seemed such a terrible idea when he'd suggested they go into work together.

He'd brought in a change of clothes he'd somehow conveniently found in his truck, grinning at her raised eyebrows, and had then insisted they should shower together again, to save time, of course.

When he'd offered to drive them both to work, she'd been befuddled from all the kissing and shower shenanigans and had agreed without even a second thought.

They'd walked into work holding hands and she hadn't even realized why people were smiling and giving them strange looks until they were halfway through the lobby. By then, it was too late, of course, so she'd just shrugged and held his hand all the way up to their floor, where they'd parted ways outside her office, but not before Jack had rocked her world with another of his wickedly hot kisses.

The rest of the day was busy, but not so busy that practically every witch in the building didn't find time to come visit Samantha's office for the scoop on her unexpected romance with Jack Saunders.

Of course, the first to demand answers was Meredith, followed immediately by Serena and then their mother.

"Really, Samantha, I'm completely shocked. I would expect this behavior from Serena, but not from my sensible daughter." Elizabeth was already speaking when she marched into Samantha's office around mid-morning.

Samantha was of the opinion this timing wasn't by accident, for Serena was already in her office, grilling her for details. "Oh? To which behavior might you be referring, Mother?"

"Flaunting your romance with a co-worker? Ring any bells?"

"Were we flaunting it?"

"I heard he kissed you right outside your door." For a moment, Elizabeth looked disappointed. "Was that just a rumor?"

"Oh, no, Elizabeth, that was truth." Meredith walked in and shut the door behind her. "I had a ringside view of it all."

"Meredith!"

"Oh, come on, Samantha. You cannot possibly expect me not to share such utterly fascinating news."

"And I heard they arrived in Jack's truck, *together*," Serena said.

Elizabeth gasped, but to Samantha's ears it wasn't so much a shocked gasp as an excited one. "Samantha! Is this true?"

"Well—"

"I heard they were holding hands in the lobby," Meredith said. "And in the elevator. And all the way through the offices to Samantha's door. I can definitely vouch for the last bit. They *were* holding hands while kissing. It was sweet. And *hot*."

"Oh, Samantha, this is marvelous," Elizabeth exclaimed. "You and Jack Saunders. I've always liked him, you know."

"Mother, we're just—"

"How are the kittens?" Meredith asked.

Serena and Elizabeth both gasped. This time, the gasps were definitely shocked.

"You got kittens?" Serena asked.

"Meredith!"

"What? It's not like it's a big secret. Everyone knew Jack left here yesterday to meet you at the Pet Emporium."

"I didn't," Serena said.

"Neither did I," Elizabeth said.

"Well, everyone who was around when Samantha called and asked for him knew."

"What did you need Jack for?" Serena asked.

"His truck."

"She bought a giant cat tree," Meredith confided.

"Meredith! How do you even know that?"

"I made Jack promise to text me all the details. He even sent me a couple pictures."

"What? When did he take pictures?"

"These I have got to see," Serena said.

Meredith grinned. "I'll be right back." She opened the door and hurried out to get her phone.

"You adopted kittens?" Elizabeth asked.

Samantha shrugged. "I found three of them abandoned in the parking lot when I left yesterday. I couldn't just leave them, so I went to the Pet Emporium to get some cat food and things and—"

"And she bought a cat tree, so she needed Jack's help to get it home. See?" Meredith came back into the room and held out her phone to Elizabeth.

Serena and Samantha both leaned over to see.

On the screen was a picture of Samantha sitting on the couch with all three kittens. Midnight was sitting on her shoulder, playing with her hair while Shadow was chewing on her jeans. Samantha was holding Smoky in the palm of her hand and was in the process of kissing him on the nose.

"Awww," both Serena and Elizabeth said at once.

"They're so cute," Serena said. "I can't believe you didn't call me."

Samantha grinned. "Why would I call you? You drive a Prius."

"Hey, there's nothing wrong with my car."

"Sure, but it wouldn't fit the cat tree."

"I guess not." Elizabeth had advanced the photo and was now staring at the ginormous cat tree Samantha had purchased.

Serena burst into laughter when she saw it. "Let me guess. Were you pretending even while buying this that you were going to give the kittens away, find someone else to adopt them, not keep them for your own?"

Samantha scowled. Her sister knew her too damn well. "I might have given them away. You never know. I still might, in fact."

"Awesome. Then you can give them to me," Serena said.

"I'll take them if Serena won't," Meredith offered.

There was a long pause, then Elizabeth said, "Well, don't look at me! I'm allergic to cats."

"Yes, we know, Mother," Samantha said. "It's why we couldn't ever have any growing up. And forget it—I'm keeping all three of them."

Serena let out a hoot of laughter and Elizabeth grinned. "See there. Didn't I tell you girls that once you were all grown up, living on your own, you could have as many pets as you wanted? And Samantha's chosen three! Isn't that wonderful?"

"Actually, it appears she's chosen a fourth," Serena said dryly. "And his name is Jack."

"Serena!"

"Did I hear someone calling my name?"

The four women turned to see Jack leaning against the doorframe, that sexy grin on his face again.

"Oh, my," Meredith whispered.

"And now we know why you were so quick to ask for Jack's help," Serena muttered.

"You don't have a single clue," Samantha said. "Here." She handed over her phone to Meredith. "I bet he didn't send you that picture."

Meredith accepted the phone, glanced down, gasped, then passed it on to Serena.

Samantha grinned.

It really was an excellent picture. She'd taken it of Jack when he was sitting in her bed watching TV. Dressed only in his boxers with all three kittens cuddled against his naked chest, one strong arm cradling them there, he was the epitome of sexiness.

She reached Jack and grinned up at him.

"What's up?"

"Gossip is rampant. Everyone's talking."

Jack grinned. "Good. Now everyone knows you're mine." He leaned over and kissed her, then murmured in her ear. "You ready to try another casting?"

Samantha jerked back, horrified. "Here? No way."

"You said you'd try again tomorrow. It's tomorrow."

"But not here!"

"Why not? Here's where it all went wrong, right? What better place to try again?"

"What are you talking about?" Serena asked.

"Samantha cast a cleaning spell yesterday."

"Jack!"

"Really? Did it work?" Elizabeth asked.

"Of course it didn't work. My spells never work. You know that, Mother."

"Actually, it worked just fine." Jack explained what had happened and that he wanted Samantha to try again.

Samantha glared at him.

"He's right, Samantha. It really does sound like you've got a lot more control than you once did," Serena said. "Maybe the curse has cured you. Maybe your magic will finally respond the way it should."

"I do not cast curses, young lady," Elizabeth snapped.

"Of course not, Mother." Serena rolled her eyes.

"Jack thinks we should be able to control our magic because we're over the age of majority now," Samantha told her sister.

Serena made a face. "Eh. You know that hasn't worked out so well for me."

"I know, I explained that, but he thinks it requires us both to try."

Serena shrugged. "You know I'm always up for some magical shenanigans."

"Oh, dear." Meredith started edging toward the door.

Samantha snickered. "See, Jack? Even Meredith knows this is a bad idea."

Chapter Twelve

"I DON'T UNDERSTAND what went wrong," Jack said later that night.

Samantha wasn't really listening. She was too comfortable in Jack's arms and was enjoying the sight of their legs propped up on the coffee table side-by-side.

So many evenings, she'd ended her day this exact same way. Sitting on the couch, legs propped up on the coffee table, the television's volume on low as she pondered the events of the day and made plans for the next one.

Tonight, however, she wasn't alone and her thoughts were not of the next day, but of how wonderful it felt to simply be in the moment with Jack.

Not to mention the kittens, who were sprawled across both their laps, in perfect, purring contentment.

"Samantha?"

"Hmm?"

"What do you think went wrong with your casting today?"

"I told you. Serena's magic and mine are combustible when we're together. I mean, the magic's explosive when we're on our own too, but it's so much worse when we're together."

"I can't get the look on your mother's face out of my head."

Samantha giggled. "Well, she *was* wearing one of her favorite dresses."

"I'm still at a loss as to how the ink from the copier down the hall managed to explode all over her inside your office. It makes absolutely no sense."

"Well…"

"Hold on a minute." Jack tilted Samantha's chin up and examined the expression on her face. "You know something." He dropped a kiss on her lips, murmuring against them, "Spill it."

Samantha grinned. "I'm pretty sure Serena was getting a bit of revenge for the spell casting. I could be wrong, but she has been known to be a bit devious in her payback schemes."

"Interesting. Remind me not to get on her bad side."

Samantha chuckled.

"So I know you haven't been using your magic since the asshat incident, but did Serena gain any control once you two hit your majority?"

"Not really. As far as I can tell, nothing changed for her at all, magically speaking."

"So what exactly did your mother cast Serena's way then? Because I'm sure it wasn't abstinence."

"No, that was just Serena being overly dramatic. Mother cast restraint upon her."

"Huh. Do you know why?"

"Probably because Serena never thinks before she acts. She's too impulsive and it manifests itself in her castings."

"So one twin has been rigidly controlling her magic." Jack tightened his arm around Samantha, making her feel as if he'd enveloped her in a giant hug. "While the other's been reckless with it?"

"Pretty much."

"But you're not holding yours back anymore."

"Well, I'm not exactly using it, but it's no longer buried either. Something that is entirely your fault, mind you, so if the house collapses around us tonight while we're sleeping, just remember—you have only yourself to blame."

Jack let out a bark of laughter. "I'll keep that in mind. If the house is going to collapse, though, there are a few very important things we should take care of first." He scooped the kittens off their laps and settled them onto the cushion beside him, then surged to his feet, hauling Samantha with him.

"What things?" Samantha demanded.

"They're all in the bedroom." Jack waggled his brows at her, then swept her into his arms and strode for the stairs. He caught Samantha's lips with his own, swallowing her giggle and setting her senses ablaze.

By the time they reached the bedroom, Samantha's body was on fire. "Jack," she murmured his name as he tumbled her onto the bed and proceeded to incinerate all of her worries in a number of deliciously wicked ways.

Long and wondrous hours later, Samantha staggered across the room, leaving a relaxed and naked Jack behind as she headed to the bathroom to brush her teeth and get ready for bed.

She was reaching for her toothbrush when she registered what she was seeing. That morning, the only things on the counter were her toothbrush in a toothbrush holder, her curling iron and dryer, and some makeup.

Now intermingled with her things were some razors, shaving cream, aftershave, a comb and in that holder where her lone toothbrush had once stood, there were now two, leaning toward each other.

She stared for a long moment before stepping back into the bedroom and opening her closet door. There she discovered a portion of her closet now housed a number of dress shirts and suits, as well as some very large shoes.

She whirled and stomped to the dresser, noticing for the first time, cufflinks had joined her tray of jewelry sitting there. A quick exploration of the drawers showed that some of Jack's clothing had also infiltrated the dresser.

She whirled to face Jack who lay on the bed, grinning at her.

Oh, that sexy grin. It drove her absolutely mad!

Mad with lust, truth be told.

"What's going on?" She demanded, hands on hips. "What's the deal with all your things?"

"Well, you did offer to move in with me yesterday."

Samantha gasped. "I most certainly did *not*!"

Jack gave her a crestfallen look. "How soon you forget. Don't you remember we decided it wouldn't be right to uproot the kittens so soon after bringing them here? I'm sure that's why we decided not to move to my place. After all, we'd already moved in the cat tree."

"What are you talking about?"

"Yesterday. You offered to move in with the kittens."

"What—you—oh!" Samantha really wanted to keep up the outrage, but honestly, it was all she could do not to laugh. He was just so outrageous, she couldn't stay mad at him. Besides, the truth was, she loved seeing his things mixed with her own. That didn't mean she wasn't going to give him a hard time about it, of course. "If I remember correctly, you said in that same conversation that it was too soon!"

"Sure. But that was yesterday. It *was* too soon back then."

"And today isn't?" Samantha asked dryly.

"Exactly!"

"Okay. Sooooo…" Samantha drawled the word out. "What? We're living together now?"

Jack's grin widened, something she wouldn't have thought possible a minute before. "I thought you'd never ask." He bounded from the bed and swept her into his arms for an intense and devastating kiss. "I accept."

"That's not what I meant, you Neanderthal." Samantha whirled away and stared around her. "How did you even get your stuff in here without me noticing? We've been together non-stop since getting off work and you couldn't have come in earlier because you don't have a key!"

Jack let out a chuckle. "I can't believe you're asking me that."

"Well, I am. Answer me please!"

"Samantha. Sweetheart. Love of my life. I *am* a witch."

She tried really hard not to laugh, but she just couldn't help it. He was so damn incorrigible. "You just wait, Jack Saunders. Vengeance will be mine!"

Jack chuckled, scooped her into his arms and deposited her back on the bed, following her down, so that he was braced above her. "If your revenge is anything like what happened to your mother today—" he gave her a tiny kiss at the corner of her mouth— "I'll definitely be on my guard." He gave her another tiny kiss on the opposite corner.

"Good."

He kissed her again, this time fully on the lips. He lingered there a moment, then pulled back to stare into her eyes. His grin was gone and a somber expression was in its place. "So, are you okay with this?"

It was a good question. *Was* she okay with it?

Samantha thought about that for a moment.

How she'd felt staring at their legs propped up next to each other on the coffee table, the feel of his fingers playing with her hair as they cuddled on the couch and talked about their day.

The sight of him cradling the kittens against his naked chest in her bed the night before.

The kittens he'd refused to take off her hands, forcing those bonds to deepen, kittens who even now had managed to claw their way to the top of the bed and were settling on the pillow next to them, their purrs filling the room and making Samantha's heart contract with joy.

The glory of waking to Jack's kisses, of sharing coffee with him in the morning.

After a long day at work, entering a house that felt like a home and the wondrous possibility of never having to go to bed alone again.

The different ways he kissed her—passionately, tenderly, lovingly— as if she were the only thing in the universe he saw in that moment.

Their toothbrushes together, his socks mixed with hers, his shoes on her closet floor.

Jack calling her the love of his life.

"Samantha?"

She leaned up and kissed the worried look from his face. "Jack. Sweetheart. Love of my life. I am very much okay with this."

Jack's eyes lit up, he settled more heavily over her and captured her lips in a heated, passionate, *wicked* kiss. Long moments later, he pulled back to stare into her eyes. "Tell me you meant that."

Samantha smiled up at him. "I meant it." She cupped his cheek with one hand, lifted up and kissed him again. "But don't think you're off the hook just because I've fallen in love with you. You're just lucky Serena and I never achieved synchronicity because I guarantee the results for you would not be pretty."

Jack chuckled, then rolled them away from the kittens so that he was on his back and Samantha was stretched out on top of him, her head resting in that perfect spot on his shoulder, a spot she imagined had been created just for her. "Seriously though, you shouldn't give up. Maybe once Serena learns some of that restraint you're so famous for, you'll both find your magic more manageable."

Samantha couldn't even begin to imagine such an eventuality. "Do you really think it could possibly be that easy? We tried for years to work together, to gain that sense of synchronicity everyone talks about." She grinned as the three kittens realized their humans had moved away from them and bounced across the pillows to settle next to them again. "Our three cousins achieved it easily, but not us. No, we're still casting spells that resemble those from our teens!"

"Are your cousins triplets?"

"No, which is what makes it so infuriating. They're not even triplets and they achieved what we couldn't. Okay, so they're really close in age, barely a year between each of them, but that shouldn't have made a difference. They're drawing from separate wells, which makes what they've achieved almost impossible."

"You think them achieving synchronicity from separate wells is more difficult than the two of you achieving it from just one?"

"Well, of course. It's so rare."

"Just because it's rare doesn't mean it's impossible and it's much more easily achieved when the magic of one isn't intertwined with the magic of another."

"If you say so, but—"

"But nothing, Samantha. There's a reason twins and triplets are so rare among witches. Sharing a well with another witch is incredibly challenging. I'm not surprised it's been a struggle."

"Knowing that doesn't make it any easier to deal with." Samantha thought about it for a moment. "Maybe you're right though. Maybe bottling up my magic somehow made things worse. It's just—I could have really hurt someone that day. I *did* hurt Maurice, badly enough that he may never enjoy sex again."

"Serves him right," Jack growled.

"I mean, I don't disagree, but—"

"But what? From what I understand, he had his hands on you without permission, and after he was fired, it came to light that he'd been harassing women in the office for years. He deserved a lot more than he got."

"Okay, but the point is I wasn't in control and because of that, my magic caused a lot of damage." Samantha propped herself up on Jack's chest, so she could look him in the eyes. She wasn't sure he truly understood how dangerous that situation had been. "I was just lucky that only Maurice was hurt."

"I don't think that was luck, Samantha. You're a good witch, one who cares about people, which means your magic had no reason to attack anyone but Maurice, and in his case, it was absolutely self-defense. To me, that says you had perfect control of your magic. You were probably scared and angry and your magic difficult to control, but you still managed to direct it toward things instead of people. Give yourself some credit."

"I suppose. I just—I hate never knowing what chaos will result from a casting. I cannot stand the lack of control."

"Then maybe we should encourage Serena to surrender to the power of your mother's spell. Now that you've loosened the reins a bit, the only thing holding you back may be Serena and her refusal to do the opposite."

"What do you mean?"

"It sounds like Serena needs to *tighten* the reins. If the two of you could somehow work together, to control the well, who knows how powerful your castings might become?"

"Yeah, well, good luck with that. Serena's not going to give in to the spell anytime soon. Our mother was so out of line with that casting."

"Maybe, but honestly, I feel as if I owe your mother a huge debt of gratitude. I have no doubt it's her spell that encouraged you to give us a chance."

"I don't know, Jack. Her spell supposedly cast recklessness my way. That doesn't exactly say good things about you. After all, it implies I had to be reckless to take a chance on you."

Jack grinned. "Well, reckless for you, my dear, is still pretty damn cautious for anyone else."

"Hey!"

"If the shoe fits." Jack hitched up a shoulder in a half-shrug, then rolled them away from the kittens again, settling on top of Samantha and kissing her long and deep. He pulled back and stared into her eyes. "All I'm saying is, whatever power brought us together, I'm eternally grateful."

He kissed her again and as the heat of his kiss devoured her senses, Samantha's last coherent thought was that she too was grateful for the spell of recklessness that have given her the courage to go for what she'd always wanted: her wickedly sexy Jack.

PEPPER McGRAW

**Serena's magic is often a hurricane of chaos.
She likes it that way.**

Serena Covington loves her life. It's full of fun and adventure and she's never bored. Of course, her spontaneity does sometimes cause her spells to go awry, but Serena figures a happy life full of fun is well worth a bit of chaos every now and then.

Unfortunately, when a spell curses Serena with restraint, it wreaks havoc on her love life, which means her planned seduction of the ultra-sexy Neil Beckett is now permanently on hold. Except Neil himself doesn't seem to have received the memo.

Under ordinary circumstances, Serena would be thrilled to succumb to Neil's charms, but now she has to wonder whether he's pursuing the real Serena or the new and improved (i.e., boring and restrained) one. If that's the case, Serena knows the relationship is doomed from the start, for when the spell wears off, so too will the romance.

Chapter One

UNBELIEVABLE!

Serena kept a firm grip on the panic inside until she reached her office where she could close the door and collapse on the couch there.

She couldn't *believe* her mother had the nerve to curse her with her twin's restraint!

So what if Serena's magic was a little wild and untamed? At least she tried to use it, unlike Samantha, who pretended she wasn't a witch at all!

This was a disaster.

And the timing was horrendous.

She'd been planning this evening for months.

Tonight was the big fundraising event for the community center and Neil would be at the event, ripe for seduction.

She'd peeked at the guest list and knew he was attending alone this year, which meant the field was clear for her to work her wiles on the man.

She'd been lusting after him for years and was determined to get him out of her system, once and for all.

If she could just have one night with him, she was sure she'd get over this ridiculous crush and be able to move on with her life.

Not that she'd put it on hold or anything while waiting for him to succumb to her overtures. A woman had needs, after all, and Serena quite enjoyed the single lifestyle and the many, varied (sexual) pleasures it offered.

Lately, though, every time she hooked up with a man, she found herself fantasizing that he was Neil, which was really putting a crimp in her style. What man wanted to be a stand-in for another and what woman wanted to feel as if she was just going through the motions while waiting for the man she lusted after to notice her?

Unfortunately, whenever they ran into each other around town, Neil acted completely uninterested, which she couldn't even understand. How could he not notice the intense, sexual attraction that burned between them every time they met? Even more importantly, how could he not want to explore it?

Since it seemed impossible he *wouldn't* want to explore their attraction, Serena was convinced he couldn't possibly be as uninterested as he pretended, and so, she'd decided to give him one more chance.

Tonight. At the event.

The only wrench in the works was her mother, who had just cursed her with restraint, the last thing she needed when plotting seduction!

* * *

Why in the witchy world Neil had agreed to cover the community center event for Joe, he had no idea. He usually covered the crime casting beat, but when Joe had asked, Neil hadn't even hesitated.

He blamed Serena.

The woman messed with his equilibrium in every single way and just the chance of running into her was enough to make him accept an assignment he knew little about.

Oh, he attended the center's fundraiser every year as a means of giving back to the community, so he knew some things about the center, specifically its mission that focused on young witches, but he didn't know much beyond that.

He'd certainly never visited, which was a problem since the assignment was to write about the changes the center had made over the last year. So he spent an hour researching the Covington Center and its history, just to make sure he knew what to expect, before heading to the press event.

From his research, it sounded like the center was more Samantha's project than Serena's, which meant she probably wouldn't even be there.

Which was a good thing.

He really didn't need to get involved with someone who made flirting an art form and who clearly had no interest in committing to a relationship.

He'd considered a one-night stand, something she clearly specialized in, but Neil knew himself well enough to know that one night would never be enough, and so he'd avoided her as much as possible.

Unfortunately, that wasn't really working anymore. He was obsessed with the woman and he was starting to think that indulging himself might be the only way to save his sanity.

And so, here he was, charming his way into the community center a good hour before the press event was scheduled to begin, on the off chance he might see the object of his obsession.

Unfortunately, he didn't see Serena among the mass of people swarming the center. There were kids and teens everywhere, all of them with name tags on. From what Neil could tell, they were there to help with tours for the press later, but in the meantime, were just hanging out, waiting for things to get started.

To Neil's surprise, he heard Serena's name several times as he wandered through the crowds. Of course, he stopped to listen every single time. After hearing the first story, followed by several more just like it, he came to the conclusion that Serena was something of a legend at the Center, all because of her inability to control her castings.

And perhaps due to her charms as well.

After all, the boys seemed quite taken with her.

Then again, so did the girls.

Neil was smirking at the latest tale when Samantha showed up, Jack at her side. Those two had a rather contentious relationship, so Neil was rather surprised to see them together.

Still no Serena though.

This would be more aggravating if it weren't for the fact that he was learning so much about her just by being there.

He was really quite impressed by some of the disasters she'd allegedly caused with her magic. He particularly enjoyed the story of her attempt to decorate the common rooms for All Hallow's Eve. Apparently, she'd accidentally cast them full of genuine cobwebs, causing a veritable infestation of spiders. According to one witness, it had taken seventeen witches to undo her casting and return the center to its spider-free state.

Neil rolled his eyes at that number. He imagined the story had been embellished over time for surely no accidental casting could possibly be so strong as to require *seventeen* witches to undo it.

Not that he was surprised to hear about any accidental casting that involved Serena. As a member of the press, Neil was well aware of her legendary castings, including a rumor that she'd once caused a ten-block grid electrical failure. That rumor had never been confirmed, of course, but he wouldn't put it past her.

Still, he was surprised the Center allowed her to cast magic within its walls with so many impressionable children and teens wandering around. It actually sounded rather dangerous to him.

Thinking he might have to explore that subject further, Neil headed for Jack, intending to tease his buddy about the way his eyes were following Samantha around the room, but stopped when he heard Serena's name spoken again.

"You should come to group." A teen, Kyle according to his name tag, said to another. "Serena's really good at coming up with exercises to help us control our castings."

"I don't know." The second boy, Max, looked doubtful. "She's kind of—"

"Hot," a third teen, Jonathan, said.

"Intimidating," Max corrected him.

"Because she's hot," Jonathan said again.

Neil grinned. He had to agree. Serena was definitely hot.

"She's nice," Kyle said. "She really wants to help. It's why she started the casting group in the first place, to help us better control our magic."

"I don't need yet another magic class," Max said.

"Group's not like our regular school classes," Jonathan said.

"Exactly," Kyle said. "Serena comes up with all these fun activities and exercises, games to play and stuff. Half the time I don't even realize I'm using my magic. I mean, I know I am, but it's not like when I'm in class and I'm really concentrating. It's more natural."

Huh. Maybe this was why she was allowed to cast inside the center. She was helping the teens with their casting control. He would never have expected it of anyone who had difficulty with their own magic, but especially not of Serena.

"She really helped Logan," Kyle said as Neil started to walk away.

"Isn't he still in juvie?" Max asked.

Neil froze.

"He just got out a couple days ago," Kyle said. "Serena helped him meet the requirements."

"He got his powers under control that quickly?" Max asked.

"With Serena's help, yeah."

Interesting. Did that mean Serena was also volunteering at the Juvenile Detention Center?

The more Neil thought about it, the more convinced he became there was a story right here at the community center and possibly at the detention center as well, one that could add depth to his work on the crime casting beat.

The rest of the afternoon flew by, with the press conference outside followed by a tour of the center, and through it all, Neil's thoughts kept circling back to the story he was already constructing in his head. Oh, he'd go ahead and write the story he was covering for Joe, but as far as he was concerned, this had just become a much bigger story indeed.

He pitched his idea to Kerry Simmons, the director of the center, and she was delighted at the possibility of some additional free press. Bonus—he'd be spending time with Serena while working.

Assuming she agreed, of course, but he couldn't imagine why she wouldn't.

By the time he walked into the hotel later that evening, he was feeling quite optimistic. He'd handed in the story for Joe and had a long list of questions for both Kerry and Serena. He also had an outline of where he thought the story might go, depending on their answers to his questions.

Even better, to write this story, he'd have to spend some quality time with Serena.

He was congratulating himself on how brilliant this plan was when he caught sight of Serena for the first time that day.

She'd just stepped out of the main ballroom where the event would be taking place and was striding across the lobby, eyes on her phone.

Every step she took gave him a glimpse of one luscious thigh.

He was mesmerized.

She'd almost reached him when he realized if he did nothing, she'd probably pass him by without even noticing him.

A quick step to the right ensured he was in her path and two seconds later, he had his arms full of lush, exquisite Serena.

* * *

Serena realized one second too late, there was someone in her path. Before she could do anything about it, though, she'd collided with the poor, unsuspecting witch.

A male who caught her in his arms and smelled divine.

She recognized that scent.

She pulled back a little and was both thrilled and mortified to realize Neil Beckett held her in his arms.

"Serena." His voice gave her a shiver. "You okay?"

She nodded and pulled away. "Of course. So sorry. I wasn't watching—"

He grinned that lopsided, ridiculous grin of his, showcasing one adorable dimple, and her heart thumped.

"I'll never complain about a beautiful woman landing in my arms."

Was he flirting with her? Neil never flirted. What was going on here? She hadn't even had a chance to work her wiles on him yet.

"So where were you headed?"

"Oh, um, nowhere important." She didn't actually remember. She was pretty sure she'd been on a mission for Samantha, but at the moment, she couldn't remember a damn thing about it.

"I'm surprised you're here so early," Neil said.

Serena smirked. Him and everyone else. "Yeah, but that's not the surprising part."

"Oh?"

"Samantha was *late*."

"No way."

"Yep. I actually beat her here."

"Impossible."

"I know, but that's the rumor."

Neil chuckled. "And did you start that rumor yourself?"

A tiny giggle escaped. "Well, just because it's a rumor doesn't mean it's not true, and frankly, it's so momentous an occasion, *someone* had to make sure it wouldn't be forgotten."

He laughed.

"I should go. I'm supposed to be... doing something for Samantha."

"And I'm supposed to be meeting Jack for a drink before dinner." He smiled. "Save me a dance later?"

Serena gulped, then nodded. "Definitely."

"Excellent." He leaned forward, kissed her on the cheek, and murmured in her ear, "You look exquisite this evening, Serena." With one last squeeze of her hands, he continued on his way.

Serena swung around and watched as he crossed the lobby and disappeared into the hotel bar.

Dear goddess of all divine creatures, he had to be the sexiest of them all.

Chapter Two

SERENA HAD SURPRISED even herself when she arrived at the event early, though running into Neil in the lobby was an unexpected side benefit.

She usually timed her arrival to coincide with the dancing and flirting portion of the evening, which typically didn't happen until after all the speeches had been given and dinner had been served.

Arriving on time, let alone early, was guaranteed to have her bored out of her mind, not to mention the possibility of being conscripted into work, which wasn't the point of these events as far as Serena was concerned. They were supposed to be fun, after all, something her sister never seemed to quite understand.

In Samantha's world, even though everything had been thoroughly planned in advance and the event manager was fully capable of handling anything that came up during the event itself, there was still no time for relaxing. Typically, she would be running around, organizing things that didn't need organizing.

Not that Serena was ever at an event this early, but she'd heard the stories of Samantha obsessing over everything from the table centerpieces to the shine of the ballroom floor.

All of this explained why Serena wasn't surprised when Samantha came bustling in and immediately put her to work.

However, what *was* surprising was that when Serena finished the initial tasks she'd been given, she returned to the ballroom to discover Samantha was just . . . *standing still.*

Sure, she was chatting with someone, but when they moved on, she didn't. She just stayed and waited until someone else approached and then chatted with them as well. She didn't seem to be at all concerned about anything or micromanaging anyone.

It was weird and completely out of character.

Maybe she was networking, but it didn't seem to be very efficient, the way she was waiting for people to come to her rather than the other way around.

If Serena didn't know any better, she'd say Samantha was *slacking off,* which she would have sworn was an impossibility.

Then again, their mother *did* cast that damn spell earlier that day. She'd not only cursed Serena with restraint, but also Samantha with recklessness. Not that slacking off would be considered reckless, by any means, but in Samantha's world, it was probably as close to apocalyptic as she could imagine.

At that moment, three men Serena knew, one of them more intimately than the others, pulled her into their group.

"Serena, good to see you." Her one-night stand from about two years back leaned over and kissed her cheek. He then introduced the other two men, but Serena was really too distracted to catch their names.

She was reconsidering her own behavior that afternoon in light of her mother's spell.

After all, for the first time in recent memory, she'd been *bored* this afternoon.

She'd even regretted not going to the center for the press event, which made no sense at all since she usually avoided the press like the plague.

Except for Neil, of course.

She made an exception for him.

Because he was just so damn sexy.

Plus, he'd never personally written a story about her disastrous castings, probably because they weren't ever of a criminal nature, which meant she could overlook his unfortunate profession.

"Don't you think, Serena?" One of the men asked, drawing her attention back to the conversation.

Unfortunately, she had no idea what they'd been talking about.

Awkward.

"I'm sorry. I wasn't—would you excuse me, please?" Without waiting for a response, Serena strode away, cringing inside.

When had she ever felt *awkward* in a group of men?

Never! That's when.

Unfortunately, Serena was starting to believe her mother's castings were actually beginning to work.

She glanced toward where Samantha had been standing.

She was still there.

In the exact same spot.

She hadn't moved at all!

This was unheard of.

Samantha should be obsessing over the food or bustling around fixing waiters' ties and generally making a nuisance of herself in her quest for perfection and—

Unbelievable.

Jack appeared at her sister's side, said something to the men there and then absconded with her, leading her out of the ballroom entirely, with, as far as Serena could tell, not even one protest from Samantha!

This turn of events was both intriguing and terrifying.

"There you are." Neil slid an arm around Serena's waist and turned her toward him, stunning her speechless.

This was the second time in one evening that he had touched her.

Once in the lobby, holding her hands and kissing her cheek.

Now here, a hand on her waist. *Both* hands on her waist.

What was he doing?

She hadn't even begun to flirt with him yet.

"Having fun?" Neil asked.

"Oh, um. Sure. I mean, not really. These things. They're never that exciting, are they?"

Neil raised an eyebrow. "If I remember correctly, that's never stopped you before."

Serena blushed. Okay, that was true. She usually took these staid events as a challenge and did everything she could to liven them up.

Tonight, though, she just wasn't feeling it.

"Yeah, but I don't usually get to these events so early. We haven't even gotten to the boring part of the evening and I'm already bored."

Neil laughed. "And what would you consider to be the boring

part?"

"The dinner. The speeches. The socializing. You know, pretty much everything that comes before the dancing."

"Right. Hopefully you'll be seated with someone—"

"Serena!" Her mother appeared out of nowhere. "I need your help. Come along."

"Oh, um—" Serena glanced at Neil, but he just smiled reassuringly. "Catch you later." She hurried after her mother. "What's so important?"

"I can't find your sister anywhere and of course, Natalie won't allow the caterers to begin serving the meal without her approval. Which is utterly ridiculous, by the way. Who does Natalie think is going to authorize payment for her work on this event? Not your sister, that's for certain."

"Please, Mother. You know how Samantha is."

"Yes. A total control freak," Elizabeth muttered.

Serena giggled, but then sobered at her mother's glare. " I suppose you already cast your tracking spell?"

"Of course I did! It ends right outside a broom closet."

Serena snickered.

"What?" Elizabeth whirled on Serena. "What's so amusing? Do not tell me you believe your sister is *inside* that closet. For heaven's sake, Serena. Your sister would never—"

"Well, no, but I did happen to see Jack Saunders spirit her away and you *did* cast recklessness upon her earlier today."

"But—*oh.*" She stopped and made a sound of frustration. "Fine. I'll find your sister. You go fix the seating."

"Fix it how?"

"Find Jack Saunders' seat and move him to our table. You'll have to move someone else away. I don't care who. Just not your sister or me."

"But *why?*"

"Because broom closets, that's why. Now go!" Elizabeth turned away, then spun back to admonish, "And don't you dare try to *cast* those changes. Do you hear me?"

Serena sighed. "Yes, Mother."

She waited until Elizabeth was out of sight before grinning. This was just too fantastic. Her mother was about to discover Jack and Samantha together. In a broom closet!

For a split second, she wondered whether she dared sneak out after her, just so she could see the fireworks, but then decided it would probably be best if she was nowhere around when everything went down. It'd be more believable when she pleaded innocence later.

Besides, she'd been given a task by her mother and she should probably get on that.

Except it wasn't quite so easy to accomplish as it sounded.

Natalie was quite adamant that all changes had to be approved by Samantha. The control freak.

Serena hated to be a bitch, but sometimes needs must. Taking inspiration from her mother's earlier comment, she glared at Natalie and said, "Do you have any idea who approves payment of your invoice for this event? Because it isn't Samantha, if that's what you think. It's our mother, Elizabeth Covington, and *she's* the one requesting these changes. So make them happen. *Now.*"

When Natalie still hesitated, Serena promised, "I'll run interference with Samantha, but I promise you she won't mind. She and Jack are *together.*"

"Oh. *Oh.* And the other change?"

Serena grinned. "Neil's with me."

Natalie nodded. "Got it." She hurried away, no doubt to cast the names on the place cards, rather than actually move them, and Serena went off to find her sister, who by now, was hopefully no longer hiding in a broom closet.

Serena only made it a few steps, though, before Neil was sliding into her path once more. "Hello again, darling."

Her eyes narrowed.

For years, she'd been flirting with this man and *nothing*.

Now suddenly, he was all 'hello, darling'? It made no sense!

"What are you up to?" She demanded.

"Me? Nothing. Though I'm pretty sure you've been up to quite a bit this evening."

What was that supposed to mean? He couldn't possibly know she'd sent her mother after Jack and Samantha. "I'm sure I have no idea what you're talking about."

"Jack's an amazing witch. Did you know that?"

Serena shook her head.

"Well, he is, and as such, he most definitely would have obscured any trace of their presence in that broom closet. So you can imagine my surprise when I saw Elizabeth, rather than Jack, accompanying Samantha back into the ballroom just now." He raised an eyebrow at Serena. "I wonder how she found them."

How Neil even knew about the closet, Serena had no idea, but she wasn't about to admit anything. "Our mother's perfected her tracking spell over the years."

"Yes, and I'm sure the fact that she dragged you away not long before your sister returned to the ballroom, had nothing to do with it."

Serena scowled. "Of course, it didn't! Now if you'll excuse me, I need to find my sister and—"

"You promised me a dance."

"What?"

"A dance."

Serena rolled her eyes. "There's no music and there won't be until after dinner when the dancing officially begins."

"True. I just wanted to remind you and to request that you guard the first dance for me."

Now Serena was beyond suspicious. Flirting, touching, even kissing and now he wanted not just to dance with her, but to claim the first dance of the evening?

She still hadn't started her seduction routine so she couldn't understand *why* he was so interested.

How could he be falling under her spell when she hadn't even cast it yet? Not that she was *planning* to cast a lust spell or anything, but this was simply incomprehensible.

Her eyes narrowed.

Could her mother's spell have anything to do with *Neil's* change in behavior?

"Serena?"

"Fine," she said shortly. "Now I really have to find my sister." Without waiting for a reply, she walked off. She needed time to think about this. Elizabeth's spell wasn't supposed to change other's behaviors, though it *was* specifically cast to change the twins'.

Samantha was definitely acting strange, not obsessing over every little detail *plus* allowing herself to be dragged off by Jack Saunders.

As for Serena, there was her boredom earlier that day, but that might have just been a fluke.

Her awkwardness with the men, though—there really was no explanation for that.

So she hadn't kept track of their conversation, big deal.

In the past she would have just laughed it off or said something outrageous to keep them from knowing she'd spaced out on them.

This time, however, she'd run away. That *was* unusual.

But was it restrained?

What did restraint *mean* anyway? Since Serena had never had it, she didn't really know what it was supposed to look like. Other than that Samantha apparently had it in droves, which wasn't exactly good news considering Samantha's personality was all work and no play, all the time, every day.

Though possibly not today, given she'd been infected with Serena's own recklessness.

And how was that fair?

Samantha was finally getting to have a bit of fun, just when Serena's was being curtailed?

Serena scowled.

Her mother had a lot to answer for with this spell.

The real question was whether Neil's sudden interest in Serena was because she'd somehow morphed into a more *restrained* version of herself.

Had she?

And if so, how would she know?

This was *not* how she'd imagined this evening going.

She'd planned to seduce Neil and then move on with her life.

The end.

But if she couldn't be sure which version of herself was appealing to him, maybe tonight wasn't the night to seduce him after all.

She wanted a night with him, yes, but only if he wanted her too—the true Serena, not some weird, subdued version of herself.

With that in mind, Serena decided she would postpone her seduction plans for Neil, and instead, would turn her attentions elsewhere for the evening.

Once that damn spell wore off, though, Neil Beckett wouldn't know what hit him.

In the meantime, she'd entertain herself by teasing her sister about a different, delectable male.

She paused a moment to contain her glee at the thought of Samantha and Jack in a broom closet together *and* to practice her surprised face. There was no way she would ever admit to giving away their hiding spot to Elizabeth, which meant she'd have to pretend ignorance while still somehow wheedling all the details out of Samantha.

She couldn't wait!

Chapter Three

AS IT TURNED out, playing innocent was all kinds of fun since Samantha turned bright red when Serena demanded to know when she and Jack had gotten together.

Samantha tried to deny it, of course, but Jack was clearly not having it, which Serena thought was completely adorable, as was his delight when she informed them he'd been moved to their table. Samantha didn't seem quite as delighted, and frankly, neither was Serena when she reached the table and remembered she'd had Neil moved there as well.

How was she supposed to abandon her seduction plans when he was apparently determined to do the seducing himself? Under normal circumstances, Serena would be delighted at his interest, but she found the timing to be entirely suspicious.

She blamed their mother.

And Samantha!

If she weren't so uptight, this never would have happened.

The worst part was that it turned out Serena's long-time assumptions about the event were entirely accurate: it *was* boring. The speeches went on forever, though Samantha's was gratifyingly short and entertaining as well. Serena was quite surprised actually and based on their mother's reaction, so was everyone else.

Finally.

A positive side effect of her mother's spell.

Unfortunately, none of the other speeches were quite so brief, nor were the other side effects as positive.

Well, except for the part where Samantha was clearly succumbing to the charms of Jack Saunders. If anyone desperately needed to get laid, it was Samantha. It didn't seem fair, though, that Samantha was finally going to get some while Serena was stuck trying to discourage the one man she'd wanted forever.

When Neil coaxed her onto the dance floor for the first time, Serena had the unwelcome thought that her efforts to discourage him were doomed. The man was entirely too sexy for his own good and he danced like a dream.

She could have stayed in his arms all night long, listening to his voice rumble in her ear, but she did her best to avoid temptation.

She switched partners as often as she could, flirting outrageously with every single one, but just couldn't seem to pull the trigger on any of them.

Even the ones who asked outright if she'd like to go home with them.

Even the few she'd enjoyed previously and *knew* they'd be good together.

Even the ones who gave her more than a tingle.

She turned them *all* down.

She blamed the inner voice Samantha had always claimed kept her on the straight and narrow, a voice Serena had always insisted didn't exist.

Well, now she had one too, and she didn't appreciate it, especially when it kept saying things like, *You have no idea who this man is. Maybe he's a serial killer.*

Even more ridiculous was when it kept nixing the men she'd slept with before. *You're lucky he didn't kill you the last time, but since he didn't, you probably won't be on your guard this time, which would be a complete tragedy since he's obviously been lulling you into a state of complacency, setting you up for the kill.*

It even tried that with Matthew, the man she kept on speed dial. He was the one she called whenever she couldn't be bothered to pick up some stranger. He did the same with her.

He was definitely trustworthy and a guaranteed good time, every time.

Still when he offered with a wink, she just shook her head and said, "Maybe next time," to which her inner voice replied, *Maybe never. He's a total player. He's probably been with hundreds of women and you're just another notch on his belt.*

Well, hello. *Serena* was a player. She hadn't counted the men she'd been with, but they definitely numbered in the double digits. *High* in the double digits. There was no reason to be throwing all those stones from inside her glass house. Besides, Matthew was a friend before he became a lover.

Yes, but that's the only relationship he'll ever want with you. Friend, sometimes lover, nothing more.

Well, who cared about a *relationship*? For goddess' sake, Serena was always the very first one on the no-relationship bandwagon! What was up with this inner voice anyway?

She blamed her mother. And Samantha.

Though it wasn't really *their* fault that married man cornered and propositioned her. For the goddess' sake. What was it about some men that made them think a woman lacked morals simply because she liked sex?

She wasn't sure which was more annoying. That her reputation had led this man to think she'd be happy to become the other woman or that she kept turning down eligible men she'd have been delighted to spend the night doing the bedtime boogie with even a week before.

She couldn't decide who she blamed more—Samantha, her mother, or the one she desired the most.

As if her thoughts had conjured him up, Neil appeared at her side and pulled her away from the idiot, not even bothering to acknowledge him as he did so.

"Whatever were you doing with that old lecher?" He demanded as he led her to the dance floor.

"Contemplating dire spells to cast upon his dick," she said sourly.

Neil chuckled. "Remind me to never piss you off."

"Exactly. It's probably best you whisked me away since who knows what might have happened otherwise." She sighed as Neil pulled her into his arms and began to sway to the music. Maybe it wouldn't be so bad to let him seduce her. She'd wanted him for years, after all.

Just let it happen, Serena, she told herself, but then that interfering bitch had to have her say as well.

What if he wants you because you're acting more like Samantha than yourself tonight? Maybe he's more interested in your sister, did you ever think of that? The thought was like a lightning bolt, killing the melting desire she'd had moments before, just from being in his arms.

"I really need some more of that chocolate mousse," she muttered. Maybe it would mellow her out.

Neil let out a soft growl, sending a shiver down her spine. "I have to say I'll never look at chocolate mousse the same way again." His voice was so deep, she had to wonder whether they were talking about the same thing.

The mousse had been an unexpected benefit to arriving in time for dinner. She'd never considered dessert when planning her arrival time in the past. Something to definitely think about in the future. "It was quite delicious."

"As was watching you enjoy it."

Dear goddess, what did that mean? She couldn't remember anything other than how rich and exquisite it was, the equivalent of an orgasm for her mouth.

Serena's eyes widened.

Yikes.

Had she said or done something inappropriate while enjoying her mousse?

Surely not.

Her mother would have *definitely* commented.

"Nothing to say?"

"Not really."

Neil chuckled. "Well, you'll be happy to know that chocolate mousse will undoubtedly become a staple in both your and your sister's diet."

Serena pulled back to stare into his gorgeous, baby blue eyes. "Whatever are you talking about?"

"All I'm saying is the two of you are *definitely* twins when it comes to that particular dessert, and there's no way Jack wasn't as riveted as I was."

"Now what exactly does *that* mean?"

Neil grinned. "Surely you've seen the sparks between your sister and Jack."

"Of course I have. Samantha's made it in her mission in life, though, to ignore those sparks. They've been going on for years." Kind of the way Neil had been ignoring theirs for years. Not that either one of them appeared to be ignoring them now.

Neil apparently agreed because he said, "I'm pretty sure that mission's a failure." He tipped his head to the side and Serena glanced over to see Samantha in Jack's arms.

Again.

Or maybe still.

Serena was pretty sure they'd been dancing all evening.

Samantha looked utterly enchanted. She didn't look away from Jack once as he led her around the dance floor.

Serena grinned. "Good for them."

"I'd rather be saying good for us," Neil grumbled, then spun them both so that Serena lost sight of her sister in the move. Then there were no thoughts left as she lost herself in the exquisite wonder of being in Neil's arms.

The longer the night wore on, the more Serena knew she was in trouble. If she didn't do something and fast, she'd be going home with Neil and all her hopes for getting him out of her system would be destroyed. How could she work him out if she wasn't even sure he was there because he wanted her?

Maybe she was overthinking things.

Well, of course she was!

That wasn't the point though.

The point was getting herself in the right frame of mind to work Neil out of her system, once and for all.

"You're quiet this evening," Neil observed.

When she didn't reply, he added, "I like it."

She stiffened. "Because I'm more like Samantha this way?"

"What? No, of course not. You're nothing like Samantha and I like that about you. You're fun and free and full of energy."

"You've never thought that before."

"I've *always* thought that, but you've also always been surrounded by a bevy of suitors."

Serena raised an eyebrow.

Neil chuckled. "Okay, tonight was no different, but somehow—"

"I was quieter, more approachable."

"Exactly."

Serena nodded. It was exactly as she'd feared. "I think I'm going to head out."

"What?" Neil stopped in the middle of the dance floor and pulled her to the side. "Why? What's wrong?"

"Nothing. I just—I need to get home. I have an early morning meeting and—well, I'm sure I'll see you around, Neil." She leaned up and kissed his cheek, then headed for their table to tell her mother goodnight.

She wasn't about to trick Neil into sleeping with some modified version of her true self. They could wait until the spell wore off and then they'd both see whether the attraction was true on his end or not.

She told her mother goodnight, repeated the same to Samantha and Jack when they walked up to the table, hand in hand, then headed out. To her surprise, Neil was waiting for her in the lobby. "Neil—"

"Hey, no worries. I just want to make sure you get to your car safely."

"You don't have to—"

"Of course, I don't. I want to." He offered his arm and she accepted it. "I assume you parked in the garage?"

"I did, though I'm surprised you realize that. Most people would assume I used the valet service."

He raised an eyebrow. "Serena Covington, allow anyone else to park her car?"

She smiled, charmed in spite of herself. "You think you know me so well, don't you?"

"Maybe."

By the time they made it to Serena's car, she was charmed all over again and thinking maybe she shouldn't allow her mother's spell to get under her skin the way it was. Then she wasn't thinking at all because when she turned after unlocking her car to thank Neil for the escort, he short-circuited all of her brain cells by leaning in for a kiss.

He gave her plenty of time to pull away, but she was quite simply mesmerized by the look in his eyes, and then either she closed the distance or he did, not that it really mattered because the result was the same, and all that was left in the world was the intensity of his kiss and the heat that shivered up and down her spine and told her *this* was no ordinary kiss.

Dear goddess, the man had skills.

* * *

Neil had the best of intentions.

Something had spooked Serena and he wasn't one to push, so all he intended to do was escort her to her vehicle and possibly bring up his plans for the story at the center.

Except when they reached her car and she turned to look up at him, all he saw were those bright, green eyes and that quirk of a smile she always seemed to have when she looked at him, and he utterly lost his head.

There was no other way to put it.

He simply couldn't help himself. He *had* to kiss her.

Of course, he went in slow, just in case she was really opposed, but unexpectedly, she met him halfway and then her wickedly, adept tongue was tangling with his and all thoughts were obliterated in a series of wickedly, delicious moments holding Serena in his arms.

They might have stayed there all night were it not for the sound of a car door closing that echoed through the garage and brought them both back to their senses.

Serena edged away and stared up at him, a dazed look on her face. "Wow."

"Agreed." He lifted a hand and brushed a bright, red curl behind her ear. "When will you be at the center next?"

"Probably next week sometime. Why? Are you going to be there?"

"Yeah. I'm working on a more in-depth story about the center. I'd love to interview you and observe some of the work you do with the kids."

Serena made a face.

"Come on, Serena. It'll be good for the Center."

"Sure, but not so good for me. I hate talking to the press."

"Yeah, but I'm not the press. I'm your friend, hoping to become something more." He waggled his brows and was gratified when she smiled back.

"Okay, fine, but what's the story exactly?"

"I heard that you've been working with the youth at the center, helping them gain control of their powers."

She scowled. "Who told you that?"

"I overheard a few conversations while at the Center earlier today and then I confirmed it with Kerry."

"Well, don't go spreading that around. People get all freaked out and nervous when they realize exactly which twin is teaching the kids control."

"But I think that's what's so fascinating," Neil said excitedly. "You're teaching these kids control despite all of your own struggles, maybe even because of them. It's probably what makes you so effective. You really understand what they're going through."

Serena shrugged. "Maybe, but I still don't want it bandied about. You know how I feel about the press, Neil. They've always vilified me, simply because I'm not willing to smother my magic the way Samantha has. You name me in your story and the press will descend upon the center like locusts. I don't know what Kerry was thinking approving this."

Neil could feel the story slipping through his fingers and scrambled to explain it in a way that would have her on board. "It's not really about you, though, Serena. I mean, the story. I want to somehow tie it to crime rates and whether we would be able to reduce crime castings if we just worked with our teens better."

She glared at the ground for a moment, then said, "All right. But I don't want my name anywhere in the story and I don't want any clues either. No mention of twins or the like. Or even my struggle to control my own magic. The minute you say that, they'll figure it out."

Neil groaned, but then nodded. "Fine. Whatever you need to feel comfortable with the story, I'm good with. When do you work with the teens?"

"Our next group meeting is Monday evening. We meet at six if you want to join us, but I can't promise the kids will want to talk to you or even participate in any activities with you there."

"Understood."

"Oh, and you have to check in with Kerry about who has parental releases on file."

"Already on it. Kerry said she'd have a list ready for me Monday."

"All right. I'll see you then." She started to get into her car, but then turned and leaned up to kiss him one more time. "And maybe we'll explore becoming something more as well." A strange look crossed her face and she amended, "Well, maybe not next week. But soon."

With a bright smile, she hopped into her car and a moment later was headed out of the garage, driving more carefully than Neil had ever seen her drive before, which made him wonder whether she was trying to impress him or if she'd finally received just one ticket too many.

With Serena, you never could tell.

Chapter Four

THE REST OF the weekend was pure frustration for Serena.

She'd expected Friday night to have a much more satisfying ending than it did.

Instead, she'd spent the entire weekend alone. The nights had been the worst, when unable to sleep, she'd spent hours tossing and turning, imagining all kinds of delightful, deliciously wicked things she *could* have been doing with Neil, if only she'd dragged him home with her like she'd originally planned.

She'd even stopped at her sister's after her Saturday morning meeting (though why on earth she'd ever thought to schedule a work meeting on the weekend, she'd never know—she blamed her mother for that too), figuring if anyone could understand her frustration, it would be Samantha.

Only when she'd arrived, she'd discovered that *Samantha* had actually spent the evening doing the mattress mambo with Jack

Saunders.

Unbelievable.

Serena had been alone in her bed with only her vibrator for company while her practically virginal sister had been heating up the night in all kinds of undoubtedly delicious ways with one of the witch community's most eligible men.

Serena couldn't decide whether she was more delighted or envious to see her sister so relaxed. Truthfully, she was feeling quite a bit of both.

She was happy for her sister, of course, but also desperate for a little bit of the same for herself.

Only with Neil Beckett, of course.

Though tempted after speaking with Samantha to track Neil down and drag him to the center where they could innocently flirt without her giving into temptation, she instead went home alone and spent the rest of the weekend bingeing on Rocky Road ice cream and Netflix.

When Monday arrived, for once, Serena was thrilled to be heading in to work.

At least it was something to do anyway.

The day was busy enough that she was actually running late when she headed for the Center.

Despite knowing it wasn't a good idea to pursue anything with Neil while under the influence of her mother's spell, Serena had spent the entire day looking forward to seeing him.

So when he was the first thing she saw upon entering the Center and his rough, sexy laugh the first thing she heard, her breath caught in her throat and she couldn't help but sigh.

Dear goddess of all sexy men, the man was utterly divine.

How in the witchy realms was she supposed to resist all that yummy goodness?

* * *

Neil was chatting with the same group of teens he'd overheard talking about Serena the day before. This time Logan, the teen just released from JDC, was with them.

Neil was enjoying listening to their perspective on the Center and its importance in their lives when Serena walked in.

Grinning, he strode toward her, exclaiming, "There you are!" Ignoring the scowl on her face, he swept her into his arms and planted a firm kiss on her lips.

She softened against him as he pulled away and he couldn't resist a second kiss. "I'm glad you're here," he murmured against her lips, then turned them both to face the teens, who looked as if they'd been struck by lightning.

"You're dating Mr. Neil?" Jonathan exclaimed.

"Go, Ms. Serena!" Logan crowed.

Kyle and Max snickered.

To Neil's dismay, Serena pulled away from him, but he was gratified to see she no longer looked irritated. In fact, that tiny, quirk of a smirk was back on her face as she said in a *very* prim voice, "My relationships are not up for discussion."

"Ooooh, relationships." Kyle emphasized the 's' on the word, laughing all the while. "Did you hear that, guys?"

"Yep," Logan said. "Sounds like more than one to me."

"Of course, I have more than one relationship," Serena said. "There's my relationship with my sister, the one with my mother, relationships with friends like Neil here plus my co-workers. Need I go on?"

The boys all groaned.

"Whatever, Serena," Jonathan said.

"Yeah, you and *Neil* didn't look like just friends to us," Logan said.

"Well, as far as you boys are concerned, that's all we are and all you need to know. So tell me. Have you three been practicing your castings?" She pointed to Jonathan, Kyle and Logan.

"Definitely," Kyle said. "I'm actually getting pretty good at controlling them now. I think."

"Excellent. What about you, Jonathan?"

"Yeah. I still struggle with distractions, but it's getting better."

"Good. And Logan, I know you've really increased your control. How're you doing with your emotions?"

"Focusing on other things has really helped."

"Give me an example."

"Well, you know how my parents are." He glanced hesitantly at Neil.

Neil had already spoken with the teens about this, but he went ahead and reiterated his promise, just to reassure them. "Remember, I won't write anything about you boys unless I have your express permission, and even then, you won't be identified by name. I will keep everything you say here in complete confidence and you're always welcome to ask me to step away if you'd rather I not hear something."

Logan nodded and Serena prompted, "So your parents were at it again?"

"Yeah. Really loud and Kaylie was scared and I was getting completely pissed off. So I focused on my breathing, just listening to the sound of it and then I got her to help me trace patterns in the carpet with our fingers. We just focused on breathing and tracing patterns and then at some point, I cast the room. I didn't even really think about it. I just did it, you know?"

Serena nodded.

"What kind of spell did you cast, Logan?" Max asked.

"Just a simple silencing spell, so no one could hear us and we couldn't hear anything outside the room. Kaylie and I played a few board games and then she fell asleep. I held the casting as long as I could and by the time it fell, everything was silent in the apartment. I guess they'd gotten tired of fighting and had gone to bed. Nothing felt so great as being able to shield Kaylie from their bullshit, though."

"Language," Serena said mildly. "And great job, Logan. I'm so proud of you."

He blushed.

Serena turned to Max. "I'm happy to see you here today, Max. Are you going to join us for our practice sessions?"

"I guess. Yeah."

"That's great. Feel free to participate when you'd like and to sit out when you don't. Nothing is required, okay?"

He nodded.

"All right then. Let's head over to the gym, shall we?"

Neil had been really intrigued the day before when the tour of the center had revealed three full-sized gymnasiums. The first two the kids had explained were for typical physical activities and games, but the *third* gymnasium was brand new. It had been paid for with the proceeds from the previous two years' fundraisers.

Of course, it was this gymnasium the journalists were most interested in, particularly because of the high price it commanded.

A cavernous space, filled with all kinds of activities and play equipment, spanning a number of different levels with obstacle courses of varying degrees of difficulty, this gymnasium was a safe space for kids to practice their castings. The gym itself was cast in such a way that no spells could escape its confines, even if the doors were opened at an inopportune moment.

The very second Neil had seen the obstacle courses, he'd wanted to play himself, and based on the conversations of his colleagues, they were interested as well.

"I can't believe the Center has no plans to use this gymnasium as a means for raising money," he murmured to Serena as they followed the teens outside through the gardens toward the gymnasiums at the back of the property.

"The thing is if we open it up to just anyone, the kids may not be able to use it when they need to and they need it more than the community does. However, our mother's trying to convince the Board of Directors to fund a free-standing gymnasium that would be open to the greater witching community. Of course, we'd charge a premium for that membership, the proceeds of which would go back to the Center, but first we have to get the Board to approve it."

"Why wouldn't they?"

"Besides the fact that it's a lot of money and they already support the Center in many different ways, including hosting and paying for the fundraising event every year?"

"Well, yes."

"Because they're a bunch of stodgy, old witches who think any good witch is one who manages to gain control of his or her magic long before they reach their majority."

"Well, that's just ridiculous," Neil said. It was the incredibly rare witch who managed to attain control before the age of twenty-five and they should know that.

"Of course, it is, but that doesn't change their beliefs one little bit."

"Don't tell me. They all managed the impossible, didn't they?"

"Well. They say they did anyway. And it's entirely possible. These are incredibly wealthy witches whose families could afford to pay for any kind of tutors and extra practice they needed. They probably all had their own private gymnasiums far fancier than this one." Samantha paused outside the doors to Gym 3 and smiled at the young ladies waiting there.

"Hello, miss," one of the girls called out, prompting a chorus of hellos from the other four.

"We've been waiting forever," a second girl exclaimed.

"Well, I"m here now and I'm certainly happy to see you five here as well." Serena unlocked the doors and led the way inside, flipping lights on as she went.

They stood inside what appeared to be a long tunnel that reminded Neil of the outer concourse of a stadium.

"Right, then, ladies and gents," Serena said. "Where shall we start today?"

* * *

Given it was Max's first time joining them, Serena wasn't at all surprised to hear Jonathan suggest, "I think you should start us off, Serena."

"Yes, yes!" Gabi exclaimed. "You start, Miss!"

Well, this was going to be embarrassing.

Then again, that was nothing new.

The only saving grace was that Serena's magical incompetence no longer had the power to drag her down into a mire of self-pity and doubt the way it used to when she was younger.

It had taken her years, but she'd eventually come to terms with the limitations of her magic, and in that process, had found a strength and resilience that infused her castings with a power few could match.

Truly, only Samantha had ever come close, and Samantha had gone the opposite route of Serena.

While Serena refused to allow her limitations to dampen her spirit or her willingness to try, Samantha had strangled every bit of power she possessed, leaving her as powerless as the non-witches.

Of course, giving free rein to Serena's power never really worked out either, with chaos being the most typical result, but she'd long since gotten used to that. And as a side benefit, for some reason, the teens absolutely loved it, which had ultimately helped in their quest for control.

The problem today, though, was that Neil Beckett, the man Serena had been crushing on for years, the man who induced more lust in her than any other man she'd ever met, was about to bear witness to the depths of her incompetence, which could very well bring to an end any hope she'd ever had of burning up the sheets with him.

Now *that* would be a real tragedy. "Okay, fine. Which obstacle?"

The teens all looked at each other, then back at her and chorused, "Water."

Of *course*, they chose the water course.

Serena glared at them, but only got grins in response.

Ugh.

They knew she was *terrible* at the water challenge, so of course, that was why they had chosen it.

"Fine," she sighed. "Lead the way."

Neil fell into step beside her as they followed the teens up the ramps headed for the third floor.

"Water obstacle, huh? Sounds interesting," Neil said.

"Sure. Interesting. More like torture," she muttered.

"Really? Why?"

"It's utterly impossible! And not just for me. I don't know a single person who's managed to get through that course. The kids just like watching me try it and fail, especially since my magic's like a freaking storm of nature on a good day and when it's near water… ugh. Watch out, that's all I have to say. Anyway. You're going to want to make sure you keep your distance. Stay behind the barrier with the kids. Unless you want to get drenched."

Neil laughed. "Okay, now I can't *wait* to see this obstacle. It can't possibly be *that* bad, can it?"

She shrugged. "I guess we'll find out, since I guarantee the kids will all want to see you try your hand at it as well." She eyed him sideways. Dear goddess, the man was sexy. He was also perfectly in control at all times, which meant he'd probably breeze through the course that was the bane of her existence in about two seconds flat.

Chapter Five

THE AIR OF anticipation among the teens was pretty intense.

Neil could tell they were excited about what was to come, which made him even more curious.

As Serena barked out orders and arranged the teens behind a glass barricade that looked down on what appeared to be a small arena, then ran down a short flight of stairs to walk to the center of that arena, he wondered out loud, "How difficult is this obstacle course anyway?"

"Extremely difficult," a young girl, Bianca he thought her name was, informed him. "I'm not ready for it yet. You have to pass a lot of the other obstacles before you can try this one."

"It's one of the hardest to pass," Jonathan said. "Only Logan's come close."

"You got pretty close last time, Jonathan," another girl said.

"Yeah, but I still wiped out in the end."

"Shh!" Kyle admonished. "She's about to begin."

Neil transferred his eyes to the arena and noticed for the first time the flooring. It had what appeared to be blue grooves winding through it.

He peered closer.

"Hold up. Are those—" he broke off as one strand of blue began to rise in a rolling wave of water. His eyes flew to Serena and for the first time, he noticed she was moving her hands in a way that was clearly mimicking the movement of the water. "Is she—"

"Directing the water?" Kyle asked. "Yes, she is."

"The object is for her to move all the water from the floor to the grooves in the ceiling," Jonathan explained.

Neil's eyes snapped upward and for the first time he noticed there were matching, empty grooves in the ceiling. How in the world? He watched in astonishment as Serena slowly manipulated one strand after another up into the ceiling.

She was *really* good at it.

He'd had no *idea* she had so much control.

All those stories, he'd thought for sure—

"Eh, just wait for it," Jonathan said with a chuckle.

"Yeah," Bianca agreed. "The task just gets harder over time. At first she only has to get one up, but then the second one while still holding the first in place. She has to get every strand up there and not let even a single one drop."

"That's impossible," Max breathed, which was exactly what Neil was thinking.

"Not really. There are some witches who can do it," Kyle said.

"Supposedly," Jonathan said. "I don't know anyone personally who's ever done it though, but these types of training courses are very popular in witching communities and Ms. Serena advocated for us to get one like this forever."

"It took her years to convince the Board of Directors," Bianca said, "and then we had to wait for the fundraising event, only we didn't raise enough money. All we could do that first year was build the building, so we had to wait another year to fundraise enough for the obstacle courses themselves. We weren't sure we'd ever raise enough to make it happen."

"But you did," Neil said.

"Eventually, but it took so long, Serena was really upset. She kept saying we needed the courses now, not in ten years when the money finally came in."

"I think she and Samantha donated a lot of money to make it happen sooner," Jasmine confided.

The teens all nodded in agreement.

Neil couldn't take his eyes off Serena as she continued to manipulate the water. One long stream of water slowly lifted to the ceiling. She kept one hand up to hold it in place as the other hand waved toward the floor and began to coax yet another strand upward.

"She's doing pretty good," Bianca said at his side.

"I don't think she's ever gotten this many up so quickly before," Kyle agreed.

From what Neil could tell, maybe half the water was above her in the ceiling while half still waited on the floor.

As the strand she was wielding settled into place in the ceiling, not a single drop falling to the floor, Serena slowly pivoted so she stood with her back to them and now faced the other half of the arena.

"Whatever you do, don't look away now," Jasmine said.

"Why?" Max asked.

"Things are going to start getting crazy," Kyle said.

"Yep," Jonathan agreed.

Two strands started flying up toward the ceiling and before they had even settled three more flew upward with a wave of Serena's other hand.

"Why's she going faster?" Max asked as four more strands lifted upward and almost collided with two more from the other side, the collision avoided only at the very last second.

Three more peeled away from the floor.

"The casting's taking on a life of its own," Neil said.

The teens all nodded.

Seven strands peeled away from the floor all at once, lifting and colliding with the ceiling in a massive show of power.

Not a single drop fell.

From what Neil could tell, there were only three more strands to go.

Three more while hundreds hung in the ceiling, held there only by the power of Serena's spell.

The final three moved so slowly, they seemed to be weighed down as they slowly climbed upwards.

At the last second, two more strands appeared, rising from somewhere so close to Serena that Neil hadn't been able to see them before. They all wound their way toward the ceiling, hitching and shaking and slowly, so slowly attaching to the ceiling.

One.

By one.

By one.

The tension in the arena was absolute.

The teens were all holding their breath, as was Neil.

He felt as if he were watching something truly phenomenal, something utterly spectacular, something he would have sworn was impossible even thirty minutes before.

The final two strands were inches from the ceiling when the tails of both collided.

One tiny drop at the end of each merged, then shattered, the strands exploding, droplets flying everywhere.

Then, as if that tiny moment was all that was necessary to break the entire casting, the ceiling exploded into a shower of raindrops, pouring down, then swirling up, racing around and around Serena's form like a giant water funnel, enveloping her form, drenching her, then peeling away, then racing back.

Again and again, the water raged in a torrential rainstorm of epic proportions.

The force of a hurricane with the power of a tornado hurtled around the room and at the center of it all, Serena stood tall, arms stretched wide, head flung back, hair flying around her like a halo, droplets clinging to every inch of her skin, the serene eye at the center of a raging storm.

Then, in one thunderous sound, she clapped her hands together and water rained to the floor, sliding back into the waiting grooves there.

Silence.

Serena turned and faced Neil and the teens.

His heart stuttered.

Her eyes in that moment were such a brilliantly bright and fierce green, they seemed to glow with the very light of her power.

* * *

Serena's heart was thundering in her ears.

For a long moment, it was all that she heard.

Then the cheering of the teens penetrated. They raced down the stairs and into the arena, where they surrounded her, almost giddy in their excitement.

"You got so close, Serena!" Bianca squealed.

"That was amazing," Jonathan agreed.

"I can't believe you got so many in place, Serena," Kyle said. "What did you do differently this time? Usually you barely get started on the second half and it all falls on you."

"I really have no idea," she said. "My well of power felt, I don't know, a little more balanced tonight for some reason."

"You share that well with Samantha, right?" Neil asked.

She nodded. "Yes, which is why we have so much trouble controlling our powers."

"That's pretty common among twins. How often do you practice together?"

Serena's heart gave a little ping, a common reaction to the opening of such an old wound. "Never anymore," she said matter-of-factly.

Neil looked stunned. "Never? But why?"

Serena shrugged.

"Miss Samantha doesn't like to cast spells anymore," Bianca told him.

"Yeah, they never go right for her, so she stopped trying," Jonathan said.

Neil wanted to ask more questions, but the look on Serena's face stopped him. This was obviously a very sensitive topic, one that hurt Serena a lot.

"Well, what you just did was absolutely amazing," he told Serena.

She'd been standing very still, almost as if tensed for a blow, but at his words, she seemed to relax. "Thanks." She looked around at the teens. "Who's next?"

In the beginning, Neil stayed back as an observer, watching as Serena worked with the teens in small groups. Eventually, though, he couldn't resist their invitations to join them in their quest to master the water course.

Unfortunately, if the teens thought he would make the difference in their ability to successfully complete the course, they were doomed to disappointment.

Though Neil had already concluded the task was a near impossible one, he realized almost immediately that he'd completely underestimated the level of difficulty.

The amount of concentration required just to move a single strand of water was phenomenal. A witch had to focus on keeping all the droplets together, not letting a single one fall, all the while moving them up into a matching groove in the ceiling.

The witch then had to focus on preventing all those droplets suspended above from breaking apart and falling, even as their attention was turned to holding together yet another strand and moving it upward into place.

No matter which group Neil joined, no matter how good they became at working as a team and holding all those droplets together, they never even got to the halfway point before everything came undone.

The entire time they worked, Serena encouraged their efforts and had them stop periodically to analyze what went wrong when a series of castings failed.

When the teams got stuck, Serena would demonstrate a technique herself, even though more often than not, it meant that she got even wetter. She never lost her patience and instead, laughed and giggled alongside the kids whenever that happened.

Neil was increasingly charmed by her infectious laughter and her merry amusement at her own inability to control her magic.

Because of that amusement, the teens seemed just as willing to laugh off any of their own missteps.

They teased each other, but in a way that was encouraging and fun, laughed whenever craziness ensued and generally enjoyed their time together.

Neil was quite impressed with the teens' can-do attitudes and their willingness to try again and again, even after repeated failures.

By the end of the evening, they were all drenched, but no one seemed to mind. The hours had been filled with laughter and as they exited the water course level, Neil couldn't help but notice that everyone who had entered earlier in the evening seemed much more relaxed as they exited.

The biggest surprise came as Neil passed through an unseen barrier from the water course level to the level below. He felt a spell wash over him and from one second to the next, he went from utterly drenched with every step serenaded by the squishing sound of his shoes to completely dry, not a single bead of water left behind.

"Wow." He froze in place.

The teens all turned, took one look at him and burst into laughter.

"We forgot to tell you," Jasmine giggled.

"Each course is cast so that no results from the magic make their way outside the course level," Serena explained. "All the water we were drenched in has returned to its rightful spot in the flooring."

"That's some powerful spell-casting," Neil observed.

"Hence the extremely high price this building commanded and why there's so much interest from the community," Serena said.

An hour later, the teens had all disbursed, headed home in rides with their parents or walking off in groups.

"Would you like to grab dinner somewhere?" Neil asked Serena when they reached her car.

She hesitated a moment, then shook her head. "I had a lot of fun, but I'm really tired. Maybe next time?"

Though disappointed, Neil murmured, "Sure," then leaned forward and opened her car door for her.

Before she could turn to climb into her car, though, he slid his arm around her waist and pulled her closer.

"I had a fantastic time tonight," he murmured, staring into her gorgeous, bright eyes.

She smiled that tiny quirk of a smile. "I did too, Neil."

He knew from his conversation with the teens that Serena usually tried to meet with them several evenings during the week. Sometimes she just helped them with homework, but most of the time, they worked through at least one obstacle at the gymnasium. "Want to do this again tomorrow night?"

Serena's eyes lit up, once more seeming to glow from within. "Sure."

Completely charmed by the wicked delight in her smile, Neil kissed her.

* * *

Serena felt as if she was operating in a daze.

All evening, she'd been utterly charmed by Neil's rapport with the kids. He'd laughed and chatted with them and generally made them all feel good.

He'd been generous with his compliments and patient when some of the teens got frustrated.

He'd not seemed to care when he got drenched more times than she could count and had just laughed off that one moment when he happened to be looking up just as one group's castings failed and he reacted too slowly to prevent the face full of water that ensued.

And now he was willing to do it all over again with her the next night.

She was so dazzled by him that when he leaned down to kiss her, she didn't even hesitate to meet him halfway, and good goddess, the man's kiss was potent!

Chapter Six

SERENA WAS STILL thinking about that kiss when she got to work the next morning to find the entire company abuzz in rumors about Samantha and Jack.

As she headed for the coffee maker in the break room, she was just in time to hear a most illuminating conversation.

"I heard they were holding hands in the elevator," one of the women, Ana, was saying just as Serena stepped into the break room.

"That's nothing," Paula exclaimed. "I heard they arrived in Jack's truck, *together*."

The other women all gasped, some perhaps due to having just noticed Serena standing there.

Serena grinned and headed for the Keurig. "Don't mind me," she said over her shoulder to the women as she set her cup of coffee to brewing. "This story just keeps on getting better and better."

Several women giggled, then one asked tentatively, "Why? Do you know something we don't?"

Though *extremely* tempted to share that she'd encountered Jack at Samantha's house when visiting her Saturday morning—a Jack dressed only in jeans and nothing else—Serena valued her relationship with her sister too much to gossip about her love life.

Well.

Okay.

She'd maybe gossip a *little*, but she wouldn't cross the line into divulging *completely* private information.

There was nothing keeping her from sharing *public* knowledge, though, now was there?

"Well, I happen to know for a fact they were both at the fundraising event Friday night."

"Yeah, but that's nothing new," Tami complained.

"And it's not like they went together," Marjorie said. Since her boss had also attended the event, she probably figured she'd know if they had.

"True." Serena smiled as she leaned back against the counter. "However, as it turns out, they were also seen dancing together." She paused deliberately. "All night long."

"No way!"

As the women began to excitedly speculate about whether this meant a true romance was blooming between Jack and Samantha, Serena collected her cup of coffee and sauntered out of the break room, mission accomplished.

Truly, the best part of this morning she decided as she headed back to her office, was the excitement and hope bubbling in the air.

Samantha, despite being such a control freak, was well-liked in the company, as was Jack, so it was no surprise most of the people Serena overheard speaking of their potential romance were excited for them both.

Though it was tempting to head to Samantha's office and immediately start grilling her on the development of her relationship with Jack, Serena knew that strategically, it would be better to let Samantha relax, thinking she was in the free and clear, then to pounce a little later in the morning, just when she was least expecting it.

With that in mind, she called Samantha's assistant, Meredith, to find out when Samantha had a break in her schedule. She then negotiated with Meredith so that she wouldn't inform Samantha of Serena's impending arrival. *Then* she called their mother because what better way to torment Samantha than to get their mother involved as well?

At precisely a quarter to ten, Meredith waved Serena into Samantha's office.

She deliberately left the door open so that Meredith could eavesdrop, one of the many conditions of her cooperation.

"So," Serena drawled out the word as she settled into one of the chairs in front of Samantha's desk. "You and Jack Saunders, eh?"

Samantha looked up startled, then upon registering Serena's words, turned bright red.

Serena let out a hoot of laughter. "Look at you! Samantha Covington, *blushing*."

"Oh, stop it."

"Well, come on, then, tell me everything."

"Only when you tell me all about you and Neil."

"Oh, him." Serena waved a hand in the air as if she could possibly dismiss Neil's sexiness in such a way. "Nothing much is going on there."

"Nothing much, is it? Too bad for you Kerry called me and told me that Neil apparently gave you a hell of a scorching hot kiss at the Center last night. I didn't even know he volunteered there."

"He doesn't. He's apparently working on a story or something."

"And you let him get near you with reporting on the brain?"

"He promised not to mention me at all. Besides, when he's kissing me, it's not like I'm thinking about anything but how incredibly hot he is."

"Serena!"

"What? You asked for details. Well, let me tell you, I have lots of details to share." She settled further into the chair, intending to torment her sister some more.

"Please don't."

"Oh, it's no trouble at all. I don't know if you've noticed, but Neil is quite the sexiest man I've ever seen."

Samantha snorted. "I seriously doubt that. Besides, you've seen Jack and I'm sorry, but he's *way* sexier than Neil."

"Oh-ho! Now we're getting somewhere. Tell me all about Jack's sexiness."

Samantha looked horrified. "I'm sure you don't need any details from me."

"Oh, but I do, I really do. That's okay, though. If you have none for me, I have *plenty* for you. Let's see. I haven't yet decided what my favorite part of Neil's body is. I'm quite partial to his—"

"I don't want to know!"

"—eyes."

Her sister slumped in relief.

"Though I must admit, his tongue is absolutely delightful, especially when it's—"

"Serena!"

Serena let out a peel of laughter just as Elizabeth swept into the office, exclaiming, "Really, Samantha, I'm completely shocked. I would expect this behavior from Serena, but not from my sensible daughter."

Meredith followed Elizabeth into the room and between the three of them, they had a grand time grilling Samantha and finding out all the details even Serena hadn't known yet.

For example, stuffy, control freak Samantha had apparently rescued three kittens the night before and Jack had helped her transport the ridiculously large cat tree she'd purchased for them, which meant by Serena's calculations, the two hadn't spent a night apart since the event on Friday.

This was clearly getting serious, which was a fantastic development as far as Serena was concerned.

Samantha seemed so much more relaxed than Serena had seen her in a very long time. She'd have to thank Jack when next she saw him.

And speak of the devil, he arrived just moments later and Serena was treated to another front-seat view of the chemistry between the two of them. It really was off the charts. She had no idea how they'd managed to ignore it for so long.

Kind of like her and Neil.

Serena got a bit distracted at the thought of Neil, which led to thoughts of his kisses, which had to be why she almost missed Jack mentioning Samantha casting a spell the night before.

Apparently, she'd caused a surge of magic so strong, it had

knocked Jack out.

Serena's eyes widened at the timing of it.

It sounded like it might have happened right around the time she'd been working her way through the water obstacle. Was that why her power felt more balanced last night? Because Samantha had finally accessed the well at approximately the same time Serena was casting spells at the Center?

Needing more time to think about this, and definitely not wanting to discuss it in front of their mother, Serena suggested that perhaps the curse their mother had cast had cured Samantha, which of course set Elizabeth off. She hated it when the twins accused her of cursing them, something she'd done many times through their younger years, though this was the first time she'd tried it since they'd hit their majority.

They really did need to teach her a lesson.

No matter what the end result, it wasn't okay for her to mess with their lives the way she had.

"Jack thinks we should be able to control our magic because we're over the age of majority now." Samantha said to Serena, pulling her back to the conversation.

Serena made a face. Such a simplistic solution that hadn't worked for her in the past.

When she protested that she'd been casting spells for years since reaching their majority and chaos was still the result, Samantha countered by pointing out that Serena had been the only one pulling magic from their shared well and that Jack had suggested pulling from the well *together* might make a difference. After all, it had been years since they'd attempted to cast a spell together by accessing their well at the same time.

Serena bit her tongue rather than say what she was thinking: that they hadn't tried in years because Samantha had given up and walked away from everything that made her a witch in the first place.

As angry as it made Serena, she understood why Samantha had made the decision she had. She just wished, as she had a million times before, that she'd been in the office that fateful day.

Once more telling herself to just let it go, Serena said, "You know I'm always up for some magical shenanigans."

"Excellent," Jack said. "Let's give it a try."

"What? Here?" Serena asked.

"Why not?" he asked.

Serena glanced at Samantha and saw nothing but anxiety written all over her.

The last time Samantha had attempted a spell at their place of work, the chaos that resulted had been extreme.

If they were going to do this, Serena needed to come up with a way to distract Samantha from her worries. "What spell should we try casting?" She asked Jack.

"Something simple, I would say."

That was when Meredith started edging toward the door, which gave Serena a brilliant idea. This really was the perfect moment to get some revenge on their mother, assuming their magic cooperated, of course, and as a bonus, would give Samantha something to focus on besides her worries.

"How about we cast Mother's dress?" Serena suggested, sending a meaningful look to Samantha, who immediately perked up, a smile transforming the expression on her face.

"My dress?" Elizabeth sounded horrified. "I love this dress. You two aren't casting any magic upon it."

"Why not, Mother?" Samantha demanded. "Don't you trust us?"

"You, I trust. Your magic, I most certainly do not."

"We won't do anything terrible," Serena said. "We'll just try and change its color. If you don't like it, you can always change it back."

"I'm not sure—" Jack began, probably concerned that Elizabeth's dress was a bit close to her body.

"I think it's a great idea," Samantha said enthusiastically.

Serena grinned. This was the best part of being twins. They could hatch out an entire plan without even saying a word to each other, in just a few seconds flat.

"Right then. Let's do this!" Serena caught Samantha's right hand in her left and faced their mother.

"What color are you thinking?" Samantha asked.

"Let's go for something simple. The dress is white, let's change it to a nice, inky black."

"Now, girls, I really like this dress. I think maybe you should choose —"

"You cast the spells, Mother. Now you get to deal with the consequences," Samantha growled, startling Serena. "We need to practice our magic and since you're the one who put us in this position, it's only right that you be the one we cast our spells upon."

"She's right, Mother," Serena said, gratified to know that she and Samantha were on the same page still when it came to their mother's interference in their lives. "Now stand very still."

Closing her eyes, she pictured the ink cartridge in the copier down the hall and then, the ink that sat inside it, just waiting to paint words on a page. She wasn't exactly sure whether Samantha was picturing the same thing, but when she went to tap into their well, she found an incredible source of magic, way more than she'd ever found there before. The surface was placid and calm, but roiling deep was a power that seemed almost limitless.

Envisioning that power scooping the ink from the cartridge and splashing it in one giant wave toward her mother, Serena's eyes sprang open at the sound of her shriek.

At her side, Samantha let out a tiny snort.

Their mother stood across from them literally dripping ink from her entire form. The ink had not only painted her dress, but everything else as well. Her hair was now an inky black rather than the silver-white of moments before. Her arms and legs were dotted as if someone had painted all of her freckles black and her feet and shoes were drenched in ink.

Her hair dripped ink, droplets falling to the floor in a cascade, as if she'd found herself in an ink storm.

"Oh, you girls!" Elizabeth shrieked. "Did I say I didn't trust your *magic*? I should have said I didn't trust the two of you to wield it!" With that, she stormed from the room, her sandals making slapping sounds against the carpet as she left inky footsteps in her wake.

The moment she was gone, Meredith peeked her head around the corner of Samantha's door, eyes wide. "What on earth happened?"

With that, the tension in the room broke as Serena, Samantha and Jack all burst into laughter.

Chapter Seven

THE REST OF Serena's day was fairly uneventful, though from what she understood, Samantha's was not. She apparently got very little work done as so many employees found excuses to show up in her office to quiz her about her budding relationship with Jack.

Serena laughed every time she thought about it.

Samantha was super private about the kind of things most people wouldn't even worry about, so Serena could only imagine how crazy some of those conversations probably went, especially the ones with women who were fairly vocal about their own dating and sex lives.

Despite her enjoyment of the gossip and seeing Samantha so relaxed *and* uptight all at the same time, the highlight of *Serena's* day didn't come until that evening when she met Neil at the center to work with the teens some more.

By the time she got there, most of the teens had already finished their homework and were ready for more spell-casting practice. To her surprise, though, Jonathan had conned one of the volunteers into supervising him and Max on the earth level. According to the volunteer, Max was ready to move on to the next challenge on that level.

The thing about the earth level was it served really well as a confidence builder. It was one of the easier levels, but had several challenges within it, challenges that varied enough to make it an interesting level to return to over and over again. Teens who had long since mastered the earth level would return to it just for the fun of playing it out, so she shouldn't be surprised Jonathan had jumped on the chance to work with Max on that level.

This should be interesting, though, because the only candidate currently available for Max to work through the next challenge with, and thus test out his newly developed skills, was an unsuspecting Neil.

* * *

When Neil arrived at the center, Jonathan and Max both made a beeline for him.

"Yo, Mr. Neil," Jonathan said. "Max needs a partner for the earth level. Help him out?"

Neil glanced toward Serena, who was watching with that tiny, quirky smile.

"If you're up for it," she said, "he does need a partner, preferably one who hasn't been through the level before."

"Then I guess I'm your guy," Neil said to Max.

"Yes!" Max and Jonathan high-fived each other, then took off through the Center heading for the back exit. "Let's go, let's go!" Jonathan called over his shoulder.

Serena laughed. "All right, then. Whoever wants to join us in

Gymnasium 3, we're headed out."

Neil noted Kyle and three of the same girls from the day before—Bianca, Jasmine and Lesly—were there again today. They all followed in Jonathan and Max's wake, Serena and Neil behind them.

"So, exactly how bad is this level going to be, on a scale of one to ten with ten being the water obstacle?"

Serena chuckled. "It's really not that bad. Maybe a two or a three. It's only a ten if you're claustrophobic." She gave him a quick look. "You're not, are you?"

Neil laughed. "Not even a little."

"Then you're good."

They reached the gymnasium, Serena unlocked the door and Max and Jonathan darted inside. They immediately started racing up the ramps, the rest of the teens thundering behind them.

Neil and Serena followed more slowly, with Neil starting to feel a little leery at how excited the kids were about this level. "Anything I need to know about this particular obstacle course?"

"The objective will be for you to make it through a maze, keeping in mind, the maze has certain spells that will be triggered as you move through it."

"That sounds like a pretty solitary gig. What does Max need me for?"

She smiled. "Max has already made it through the maze. His job is to get *you* through the maze."

"Huh. So what? He just leads me through it?"

"More or less."

"Sounds easy enough." Neil cast her a suspicious look. "What's the catch?"

"Basically, the maze is unpredictable. It will certainly have changed since the last time Max went through it and will undoubtedly change again, probably while the two of you are inside it. Possibly multiple times. And the main catch is that *you* may not cast a single spell. This is where Max comes in. He has to use *his* spell-casting abilities to get *you* through the maze."

"Well, that sounds like fun. No wonder you asked if I'm claustrophobic."

Serena laughed. "Actually, it *is* fun. If you ask the kids, they'll probably tell you this is their favorite level. They come back to it over and over again, despite the fact they've all pretty much mastered it, except for Max, of course."

"Interesting." Neil had to rethink that word when he actually saw the maze. It was made up of towering walls of foliage, walls that were significantly taller than him. Intimidating now seemed a better word.

Glancing around, he realized Max was the only one waiting for them at the entrance to the maze. "Where'd the other kids go?"

"Look up," Serena said.

High above them, the kids were all standing behind a clear glass wall, giving them an excellent vantage point over the maze itself.

"The ramp circles this level," Serena explained. "They can pretty much watch from anywhere along the ramp and see what's happening in the maze itself."

"Wonderful," Neil muttered. "I always love an audience when I get hopelessly lost."

Serena giggled, then turned to Max. "You ready?"

Max nodded.

"All right, head on in," she said to him. She waited for him to step inside the maze, then said to Neil, "We're going to give him to the count of ten, then you're going to follow him in. He'll be a ways ahead of you, so you'll have to listen for his voice to guide you."

Neil nodded.

"All right, you're up!"

Neil stepped into the maze and immediately felt a surge of adrenaline as the challenge of figuring out where to go became immediately apparent. There were three branches in front of him, three different ways to go and he had no idea which one to choose.

Then he heard Max's voice. "Go to the left, Neil!"

With a shrug, he quickly headed left, only to dead-end within about five feet. Huh He turned to go back the way he'd come, only to discover the maze had closed behind him.

Well, great. He was already stuck.

"Keep walking!" Max called.

"Which way?" Neil called back.

"Forward, not back!"

"It's a dead-end."

"Just walk, man!"

So with a shrug, Neil started walking toward the dead-end, as commanded. It wasn't until he was almost on top of the wall that he realized there was a gap in the hedge to the right that he hadn't seen until that exact moment.

He slipped through the gap and found himself in a large, cavernous room. Behind him, the gap sealed. He walked across the room and at about the halfway point, the wall opposite him parted revealing a single pathway.

He followed that path too.

What followed was both aggravating and fun, all at the same time.

No matter how quickly Neil walked, he never quite caught up to Max, who would call out instructions whenever Neil seemed to get stuck and didn't know where to go next. More often than not, the maze sealed itself behind him, preventing him from turning around and trying another path.

He lost track of the dead-ends he ran into, only to have those dead-ends reveal a new pathway that would twist and wind further into the maze.

Eventually, the pathway he was on began to shrink. He turned a corner and found himself facing a small entrance to what looked to be a tunnel made entirely of plants. He turned around, only to discover the maze had closed behind him. Again.

He sighed. "Seriously?"

He looked up, but the walls of the maze were so tall, no matter which way he looked, he could never see the ramps surrounding the maze, where he knew the kids were all hanging out watching.

Groaning, he stepped forward into the tunnel.

As if on a motion sensor, soft lights lit up along the pathway, guiding him up a slight incline. As he climbed, he wondered where Max had gone. Maybe he was just being led on a wild goose chase. Maybe Max had already left and was even now enjoying a nice, juicy hamburger somewhere far from this damn maze.

Unfortunately, the tunnel's roof began to slope downward, even as the floor sloped upward, which meant that eventually Neil was on his knees, hoping he wouldn't be reduced to a belly crawl next.

Eventually he reached the end of the tunnel.

Another dead-end.

And unfortunately, this time, from what Neil could see, there were no tiny gaps waiting to be found.

"Now what, Max?" Neil called out.

Max's voice came back. "Stand up!"

"Uh…" Neil rolled his eyes upward. Yep. A roof of foliage was still above him, so close he could feel it brushing his hair.

"There's no room!" He called back.

"Just stand up, man!"

Neil shrugged and very slowly, carefully climbed to his feet. As he pushed upward, the foliage parted, falling away in a complex bit of spell-casting.

Neil found himself standing on the ramp outside the maze, facing Serena and the teens, who broke out into applause and began to cheer and congratulate Max on a job well-done.

Neil put his hands on his hips and scowled at the lot of them. "Max? What about me? I'm the one who was just crawling through an imaginary, shrinking tunnel!"

The teens all laughed as Serena explained that Max had been led through the maze by Jonathan earlier that day.

"He was much faster than your witchy ass," Jonathan said, causing the others to hoot with laughter and Serena to say her oft-repeated, "Language," which they ignored.

"The first challenge is to be led through the maze by someone else," Serena explained. "The second challenge is to guide someone else through the maze using only the power of your castings," Serena explained.

"Seriously?" The incredulous look on Neil's face was classic. "So the voice I kept hearing?"

"That was me casting a projection of my voice," Max said. "I've been up here with everyone else the entire while."

"But I saw you go into the maze!"

"Also an illusion," Max said. "I couldn't hold it very long, though, so it was a good thing I got a head start."

"It was long enough," Serena said.

"Yep, long enough to fool *his* witchy ass," Kyle said, bringing about another loud round of laughter.

"We have about another hour before group is over," Serena said. "Anyone want to work on challenges three and four?"

All the teens jumped at the chance to play some more.

They divided into two teams, with Team A working on challenge three, which Serena explained was to use their casting skills to rearrange the maze, creating new dead ends and such.

Team B had to wait outside the level until the maze was complete and then had to solve the fourth challenge, which was to make it through the new version of the maze their opponents had created. They could cast spells along the way, to help them navigate the maze or even rearrange it if they got truly stuck.

Team A had the opportunity to recast the maze exactly three times while their opponents were inside. They had to work together as a team to decide when the perfect time to do this would be and how.

Neil was incredibly impressed at the challenges and at the ingenuity of the teens as Team A rearranged the maze and Team B worked their way through it, sometimes creating their own pathways to freedom.

There was a lot of laughter, especially when Team A tried to shift a wall, hoping to trap Team B inside the maze, only to have the wall break apart into a dozen tiny trolls made of leaves.

"Where did those come from?" Serena laughed.

Bianca giggled. "It was my fault. As I was helping to cast the spell, I noticed one of the leaves was in the shape of one of those troll dolls —you know the ones, with the spiky hair—and suddenly, they were all I could think about."

Down in the maze, the first team was scrambling to catch the tiny trolls, who were giving them a merry chase, hopping onto the walls and barreling through them and generally causing mayhem.

From that point, a whole lot of chaos ensued until the teens in the maze decided they were done troll-hunting and just sat down, backs against the walls of foliage and watched as the trolls played hide-and-seek among the branches and leaves of the walls that weren't impacted by Bianca's spell.

Later, when Serena gathered the teens together, they talked about everything that went well and what went wrong, including the troll-spell. As Bianca explained what had happened, Serena asked the other kids to share times when their focus had been broken as they were working on a spell and what the consequences were.

Neil was once again struck by Serena's rapport with the teens. She had somehow taken an incident that could have been terribly embarrassing for Bianca and had made it seem common, helping the kids see that these kinds of mistakes could happen to anyone. She then asked them to come up with ideas of what they could do in the future, upon realizing their focus was broken, to ensure a casting didn't go off the rails and gain a life of its own.

The kids all had great suggestions, from pulling the magic back into the well and dissipating the spell, to putting a pause on the casting and just holding the magic still until they could regain focus, at which point, they would release the casting again.

Chapter Eight

SERENA WAS COMPLETELY dazzled by Neil.

His cheerful response to the entire maze experience, his rapport with the kids, and his understanding and kindness had all worked together to make her fall just a little deeper into fascination with the man.

Once again, he'd been generous with the compliments and had encouraged the teens as they'd worked their way through the challenges.

He'd teased Max that next time, Neil would be the one leading Max through the maze, so that he could get even for Max making him crawl.

Max had assured him that Jonathan had made *him* crawl too.

Neil had laughed and exclaimed, "Good job, Jonathan," which had made Jonathan light up in delight.

Serena absolutely loved those moments—seeing how the teens responded to Neil and how patient and wonderful he was with them— to the point that her resistance was at an all-time low when Neil asked her to dinner again after they'd seen the teens off.

This time, she agreed and they met at the local Shenanigans, where they ate veggie burgers and fries, drank from a seemingly endless bottle of witches' brew and talked long into the night.

They talked about so many things, from the story he'd been working on to Serena's continuing struggles with her magic.

Neil explained why he thought the work Serena was doing at the center could be beneficial if applied on a larger scale, perhaps even reducing crime-casting rates, particularly among young witches.

Serena talked about Samantha's refusal to access their shared well of magic and how that had impacted Serena's own control.

"Does she know how much worse your control is because she's not helping to balance the well?" Neil asked.

"No, and I'm not ever going to tell her. Of the two of us, Samantha was the one most hurt by our inability to control our magic."

"How do you figure?"

"Long before we started practicing our spells, Samantha showed a need for organized surroundings. She hates chaos and gets really upset when things are out of her control. When our magic went haywire and we just couldn't count on being able to cast a single spell accurately, she really struggled. Chaos resulted from almost every spell we cast and she hated it."

"So she just shut it all down?"

"Not at first. Once we were out of school, she was biding her time, waiting for when we reached our majority. So she wasn't really using her magic, but she wasn't planning to shut it all off either. We were both hoping that reaching our majority would somehow help, but then, six years ago, a good eighteen months before our twenty-fifth birthday, she cast a really big spell and it changed everything."

"How do you mean?"

"It was self-defense, but the spell caused a lot of damage and she basically turned her back on the well."

"So she doesn't use her powers at all?"

"Not anymore. She insists she's happier without the chaos."

"Hold on a minute. Six years ago? Wasn't that when you blew that ten-block grid?"

"That's what they say."

He stared at her. "The press blamed you for the incident. Are you saying it was Samantha?"

"It was easier to let everyone believe it was me. Samantha was already upset and the truth is it was my magic as much as hers. She pulled on the well, fast, and I felt her panic and fury and my power just went to her in a surge and we blew the neighborhood's electrical grid. Plus laid out the asshole who caused the entire thing."

Neil's eyes narrowed. "Someone attacked her?"

She shrugged. "Samantha wouldn't call it an attack, but what else could it be when someone corners you, touches you without permission and refuses to let you go when you ask?"

"An attack," he growled.

"Exactly. But she doesn't see it like that. She thinks she overreacted and—" Serena shook her head. "She can't get over how easily our magic could have hurt someone in that moment. She thinks we were lucky. So she shut it all down."

"And your magic got more difficult to control," Neil guessed.

"Not at first. But later, as more time passed and she wasn't accessing the well, yeah."

"But you won't tell her because—"

"Samantha deserves to be happy."

"So do you," Neil growled.

"I am happy, Neil. I may not be able to control my magic, but it's not hurting me and I've learned to turn it to my advantage. The kids love that I can't control my castings. They relate to me and they trust me and that's really all that matters, as far as I'm concerned."

"Okay." He nodded. "I don't like it, but I do understand. So you also volunteer at the JDC?"

"Not regularly. Only when one of my kids at the center ends up there, which doesn't happen very often."

They continued talking long into the night and Serena found herself falling deeper and deeper under his spell. He was quite simply magnificent. Smart, funny, kind.

She was starting to think she no longer wanted him for a one-night stand.

She just wanted him.

No limits at all.

They left the bar as it was closing down, knowing they would both regret the late night when heading to work in the morning, but not feeling an ounce of remorse about it.

He walked her to her car and kissed her goodnight.

One kiss led to many until she thought she might go up in flames from wanting him. Finally, he pulled away and she went to get into her car, but then thought of something.

Turning back, she told him, "We don't meet for group on Wednesday nights. A lot of the kids have other commitments. However, I was thinking of going over to Samantha's after work and wondered if you'd like to go with me. Maybe we could get dinner after?"

Neil gave that half-smile of his, revealing one adorable dimple, and said, "I'd love to. Shall I pick you up at your place?"

Serena nodded.

"Six o'clock?"

"Sounds good." She leaned up and kissed him one last time, then climbed into her car and drove home, smiling the entire way.

Chapter Nine

"TO BE HONEST, I'm mostly going to Samantha's out of sheer nosiness," Serena told Neil as he drove them to her sister's the next evening.

Neil grinned. "To be honest right back with you, I'm thrilled to be invited along on this mission with you. How obvious are we going to be in our nosiness?"

"Oh, we won't have to be obvious at all. The minute Samantha opens the door and sees me on the other side, she'll know why I'm there. Of course, we're going to *pretend* we're there to meet her new kittens."

"Samantha adopted kittens?" Neil asked incredulously.

It was a valid question. Serena could barely believe it herself. "Apparently she rescued them from the parking lot at work and so, as far as Samantha's concerned, that's why we're visiting. Even though all three of us know it's not the real reason, you and I will *never* admit it.

Got it?"

Neil laughed. "Got it."

Serena couldn't have timed their arrival any better because *Jack* answered their knock.

Although she'd half expected him to be there when they arrived, she really hadn't expected him to answer the door, so was a little stunned when it happened, then entirely gleeful. This was just too good to be believed.

"Hey, Jack," Neil said while she was still processing and trying to contain her glee.

"Hey, Neil, Serena. Come on in. Samantha's on the phone upstairs. Some work call."

Again. Perfect timing.

Serena and Neil followed Jack into the condo, but Serena was instantly distracted by the living room. "Wow."

"What's up?" Neil asked.

"It's cat central." Serena laughed.

In one corner of the living room a giant cat tree now stood and scattered throughout the living room were cat toys and cat beds and— adorable—three kittens curled up in a ball on the couch.

Serena made a beeline for them. She settled next to them, which had the happy effect of waking all three of them. They immediately decided she was worthy of exploration and started climbing all over her.

Serena scooped up one of the kittens and kissed it on its nose, then cuddled it close. "I can't believe Samantha hasn't freaked about the claw marks in her leather couch." She looked up at Jack. "Or hasn't she seen them yet?"

Jack chuckled. "Oh, she's seen them, but I think she was more relieved we found the couch at all."

"She lost her couch?" Neil asked.

"Spell gone awry," Jack said. "Turned out it was on the front lawn, but we didn't know that for a while and she was a little upset because of it. After that, I don't think the claw marks really bothered her that much."

"I've decided it's the price I have to pay for being a cat mom," Samantha announced as she walked into the room. "Hi, Neil."

"Hey, Samantha."

Samantha scooped up one of the kittens, then plopped down onto the couch beside Serena. She bumped shoulders with her sister and said, "Seriously? You barely waited twenty-four hours to come snooping."

"I don't know what you're talking about," Serena said in her most innocent voice. "I'm here to meet your adorable kittens. What are their names?"

"You're not fooling anyone, you know," Samantha said. She then pointed to the black kitten Serena was holding, "You have Midnight there and this one is Shadow." She held up the second black kitten she was holding.

"How on earth do you tell them apart?" Serena asked.

"Midnight has black whiskers and Shadow here has white ones."

"You're kidding. That's it?"

"That's it."

"And the little gray one?" He was curled up in Serena's lap, purring up a storm.

"Smoky."

"I love them," Serena said.

"I know. Me too. I had no idea how happy having kittens would make me, but I'm totally in love."

Serena snorted.

"What?"

"You must be in love. And I'm not talking about the kittens."

Samantha blushed. "Yeah. Well. Him too."

* * *

The twins were simply stunning sitting next to each other on the couch.

Neil discreetly took a couple pictures of the two of them leaning into each other, their heads touching, the two shades of their very red hair, Serena's a lot brighter than Samantha's, blending together, both of their heads tilted down to stare at the kittens they were cuddling and playing with.

As he lowered his phone, Neil noticed Jack was doing the same thing.

"So, you and Samantha," he said.

"You and Serena," Jack replied.

Neil laughed. "It's pretty new. We're just feeling our way at the moment, especially since she's always been the one-night queen."

Jack snorted. "And Samantha was the ice queen, which I absolutely assure you she is not."

They both grinned.

* * *

"They're staring at us, aren't they?" Serena muttered.

Samantha giggled. "Of course, they are. We should totally call them on it."

Without taking her eyes off the kittens, who were chasing a string Samantha was dangling in front of them, Serena called, "What are you two staring at?"

"Magic," Jack said.

"Pure magic," Neil agreed.

Serena rolled her eyes.

"Not even close," Samantha said.

"And speaking of magic, are you two up to practicing together again?" Jack asked.

"Here?" Samantha exclaimed. "No way."

"Wait, what are we talking about?" Serena asked.

"Jack wants us to practice some more, like we did yesterday in the office," Samantha said. "He thinks we can learn control if we work together."

"What do you think?" Serena asked her sister.

Samantha shrugged. "I mean, yesterday wasn't a *total* disaster."

"I think our mother would disagree." Serena grinned.

"Yes, but you and I both know we cast that spell perfectly."

Neil let out a hoot of laughter. "Wait a minute. You let me believe the spell malfunctioned."

"Well, of course, it did," Serena said. "At least that's the story our mother will forever believe." She glared at Neil. "Understood?"

He grinned. "But this is wonderful! You two cast a spell together that actually worked the way it was supposed to!"

"Well, no matter what Samantha says, it wasn't *perfect*," Serena said.

"Hey, compared to the typical spells we're known for, it was perfection personified," Samantha said.

Serena laughed. "Okay, valid point, but I wasn't actually trying to paint her dress. I was aiming for her shoes. You *know* how much she loves them." Elizabeth spent a veritable fortune on designer heels every year.

Samantha snickered. "Okay, and truth be told, I was aiming for her hair because, well—"

"'A lady's hair should always be immaculate,'" Serena and Samantha quoted together, then burst into laughter.

"Anyway, I figured a terrible dye job might teach her a lesson," Samantha said.

"I thought the same about her shoes." Serena grinned at her sister.

"Well I'd say you both aimed pretty true," Neil said.

"Yes, but we still overshot our canvas," Serena complained. "Her shoes being drenched in ink wasn't as effective as it could have been, when so much of the rest of her was covered as well."

"Exactly," Samantha said.

"Even so, this is great news," Jack said. "I would imagine if you continue to work together, you'll both gain control rapidly."

"He's right. We should practice," Serena said, almost unable to believe they were actually having this conversation. Samantha had finally unsealed the well from her end and they were already seeing a difference.

"Not here," Samantha insisted. "I already almost lost my couch."

Jack snickered.

"How about the center?" Neil suggested. "It'd be an excellent opportunity for the teens to see firsthand that everyone struggles with their magic, even adults."

"That would work," Serena said. "But I don't want to take over the kids' group time with our own casting session, so it'll have to wait until the weekend."

"How about Saturday?" Jack asked.

"Works for me," Samantha said.

"Awesome!" Serena's voice went shrill at the end as something sharp pricked her ankle.

She leaned forward and saw that Smoky was attacking her shoelace, and in the process, catching her ankle with his claws every now and then.

"You are so cute!" Serena scooped him up and said to her sister, "I need one of these little guys."

"Well, you're just going to have to find your own," Samantha said. "These little guys are all mine."

Serena let out a huff of annoyance, but was secretly thrilled to hear such happiness in her sister's voice.

"I've never seen Samantha so relaxed before," she said to Neil once they were back in his car.

"Jack's a miracle worker," Neil agreed.

"Either that or our mother's spell is," Serena muttered.

"Spell?"

Serena sighed. "I'll tell you at dinner." She just hoped he didn't flip out on her.

Of course, that was too much to hope for.

"Does this mean as soon as the spell wears off, you won't want to hang out anymore?" Neil demanded over their meals.

"Seriously? Do you really think I'd be here with you right now if I didn't want to spend time with you?"

Neil shrugged. "I'm not sure. I mean, you never really seemed that interested in me before."

"Are you kidding me right now?" Serena demanded. "I've flirted with you from the moment we met. I've sent you signal after signal that I would be very interested in jumping your body and you've ignored every single one. If either of us is acting out of character due to that damn spell, it's you. You're the one who asked me to dance, asked me to dinner, all the things."

"I did that because I realized there was more to you than I ever saw before."

"And how do you figure that?"

"It's how you are with the kids at the center."

"You danced with me long before seeing me with the kids."

"True, but I overheard them talking about you when I was at the center for the press event last Friday. It was obvious from what they were saying that you worked with the kids on a regular basis. I was instantly intrigued. Then we danced and the chemistry between us is off the charts and the rest is history, as they say."

Serena smiled. "It is pretty intense, isn't it?"

"Incredibly intense."

They smiled at each other. The rest of the evening, they talked about less volatile subjects, getting to know each other better.

Later, when he took her home, he kissed her on her front porch—long, drugging kisses that left her heated and breathless and aching for more.

Thursday and Friday at work were interminable. His texts and knowing she would see him after work were the only things that made the work days bearable.

She'd be busy working when her phone would suddenly chime with an incoming text from him. It was always a cute little meme or comic, guaranteed to make her smile and brighten her day.

She'd then text him back something equally silly and they would indulge in a meme or comic war for a while before one or the other was dragged back to work and the fun would end until he initiated another round later.

They spent Thursday evening at the center with the teens as usual, then went to dinner after.

At the end of the evening, for the third night in a row, Neil devastated her senses with a series of smoking hot kisses. It was touch-and-go for a while there, but she did manage to resist the temptation to invite him home with her, exhibiting an amount of self-control she would have sworn she did not possess even a week before.

Dear goddess, the man was potent.

Friday evening, there was no group at the center, so Neil met Serena at her house and took her out to dinner and a movie.

Serena couldn't remember a single thing about the movie, she was so distracted by Neil at her side. He held her hand the entire time, gently stroking the sensitive skin on the inside of her wrist and effectively raising her desire to a fever pitch.

After, they went to dinner and they talked and laughed, sharing their days with each other and some of the most annoying work moments they'd had to deal with.

Neil's were pretty hilarious being a reporter, much more entertaining than any of Serena's stories, though he seemed riveted by every word she spoke.

By the time he drove them home, she'd come to terms with everything she was feeling. Somehow, in the course of one week, she'd fallen in love with Neil Beckett.

Fallen in love.

Something she'd never thought would ever happen to her, something she'd *planned* to never happen to her, out of the blue had blindsided her.

As they drove home in silence, once more holding hands in the dark, Serena decided if she had to fall in love with someone, she couldn't imagine a better person than Neil Beckett.

When they reached her front porch, Serena was ready. She unlocked the front door, turned to face him, leaned up for their already traditional goodnight kiss, hooked a hand in his tee-shirt and pulled him into the house with her. "You're not leaving me all hot and bothered again," she told him.

Neil grinned. "You've made me a very happy man." He closed and locked the door behind him, then swept her into his arms for a heated kiss. "Lead the way, my lady."

Chapter Ten

SERENA WOKE SATURDAY morning with a smile on her face.

A sexy, naked Neil was sprawled at her side and all was right with the world.

She shivered as memories from the night before bombarded her. She'd always assumed they'd be good together, just because their chemistry was so off the charts, but the reality had been *so much better* than she'd expected.

She now realized how foolish her expectation to work Neil out of her system had been. If they'd gotten together all those years ago, the first time they'd met, well, he'd have probably ruined her for any other man.

"What are you thinking about so loudly over there?"

Neil's rough, just-woke-up voice sent another shiver down her back.

"Just that one night will *never* be enough," she admitted.

Neil leaned up on one elbow and raised an eyebrow at her. "Were we only planning one night?"

She grinned. "Maybe back when I first met you. Now…" Serena hesitated, but then decided she'd never been shy about stating her wants before. She wasn't going to start now when it was so damn important. "Now I'm leaning more toward planning a lifetime."

Neil's eyes lit up. "Then we're definitely on the same page." He rolled on top of her and went to kiss her.

Serena flung up a hand, blocking her mouth. "No. Morning breath!"

He rolled his eyes and swept her hand away. "We can have morning breath together." He captured her lips in a searing kiss that blew every thought from her head and had their passion blazing.

* * *

"It's all your fault," Serena said hours later as Neil settled into the drivers' seat beside her.

"What's my fault?"

"That we're running late."

"Ha. I'm not the one who insisted we shower together." Not that he was complaining or anything.

"It was a time-saving maneuver, not to mention healthier for the planet. We were conserving water."

"Yes. I'm sure the planet is *very* grateful." Neil grinned. *He* certainly was. Serena had a wicked sense of humor and an impeccable sense of timing, one that had made them significantly late for their meeting with Jack and Samantha at the center. "You know, we could cancel and go back to bed." He waggled his brows at Serena.

"I'm *all* in favor of that plan." She sent him a wickedly sexy smile.

"I'm sure you are." Neil chuckled. "But no. We're getting this done." He started the car.

"I'm sure Samantha would understand. In fact, she'd probably welcome the opportunity to stay in bed with Jack herself."

"We're going." With that, Neil put the car in drive and headed for the center.

"Fine. Just try not to get in the way of the chaos that ensues."

He chuckled. "You never know. This might be the breakthrough you've been waiting for."

"What challenge do you think we should start with?" Though Serena asked the question in an offhand manner, Neil could here the note of anxiety in her voice.

"Probably not the water challenge."

Serena laughed. "Yeah. I don't think we're ready for that."

It shouldn't surprise Neil that when they got there, the center was swarming with teens, who immediately raced to Serena's side and began offering their suggestions for which challenge to try.

"Hold on, hold on," Serena exclaimed laughingly. "How did you guys even know this was happening today?"

"I told them," Kerry said as she approached. "I thought it would be good for the kids to see this."

"Thanks a lot," Serena said dryly.

At that moment, Jack and Samantha walked into the center.

"See that?" Serena asked Neil. "They're even later than us." She sent her wickedly sexy grin his way. "We totally should have gone back inside."

Neil chuckled. "Too late now."

"Oh, well," Serena said. "We'll keep that in mind for next time."

"You should totally do the water challenge together, Serena," Bianca said excitedly.

"She's right," Jonathan said. "You almost got it last time. If you and Samantha work on it together, I bet you'd nail it."

"Absolutely not," Samantha said. "I've seen that challenge and we're *not* starting there. That shit's hard."

"Samantha!" Serena exclaimed.

"What? It's not like they've never heard the word 'shit' before, right, guys?"

A chorus of "shit yeah," and "shit's my favorite word," and "holy shit, Samantha cursed," among other responses came flying back.

Neil snorted in amusement. The look on Serena's face was priceless.

Samantha grinned. "See? What'd I tell ya?"

"What's gotten into you?"

Samantha shrugged. "Blame Mother and that stupid curse."

Serena rolled her eyes. "I think I'll blame Jack instead." She glared at him mockingly. "You're corrupting her!"

Jack chuckled. "Every chance I get."

Samantha giggled. "Okay, let's get this show on the road. What level—and *not* the water level," she said to Jonathan when he opened his mouth.

"I know. Let's do Spell-Tag!" Logan suggested. "We can all play then."

"I don't know," Samantha said. "I don't want you kids getting hurt when our magic goes haywire."

"They'll be fine," Kerry said. "There are all kinds of protective spells on the gymnasium. They should keep your magic from becoming too dangerous."

"Great," Samantha muttered.

"Come on." Serena linked arms with her twin and dragged her through the center. "Let's just get this over with."

Fifteen minutes later, Neil wasn't sure this had been such a great idea after all. Everyone was now dressed in tactical vests and were armed with bows and arrows. "So what are the rules exactly? Because these arrows look dangerous."

Serena giggled. "Don't worry. They're magic arrows. They've all been cast so the spell is what hits the target, not the arrow itself."

"What happens to the arrow?" Max asked.

"It feels solid, but once it's airborne, it's just a spell, nothing more."

"Weird," Max said.

"I have to agree," Neil said. What if the arrow malfunctioned?

Not wanting to let on to the kids that he was worried, he didn't say what he was thinking, but instead asked again, "What are the rules?"

"All right, listen up," Serena called out.

The room quieted down.

"The objective of the game, quite simply, is to not get hit by spells. You can cast any spell that will harmlessly mark your victim. Remember, you're casting your carrier, which means that each arrow pulled will cast that specific spell. When you need a new spell, you'll have to dissipate the old one and cast a new one upon the carrier. Here are some suggestions: you could cast the arrows to spray paint. You could cast them to shoot baby powder. You could cast them to apply temporary tattoos. Nothing can be permanent and everything must be appropriate for this setting." She glared around the room. "Understood?"

A lot of head-nodding and "Yes, Serena," ensued.

"Good. Now as for how you win, you must tag victims using no less than five different methods, which means you'll have to be switching between spells rather rapidly. You may not tag any victim with the same method more than once. So if you accidentally tag someone with paint twice, the program will know it, and all paint will disappear from *all* of your victims."

"That's rather harsh," Max grumbled.

Several of the teens snickered.

Serena ignored them and continued. "The scoreboard will keep track." She pointed to a giant scoreboard above their heads. "It will move you up and down the list according to the number of points you have. The first column tallies every time you hit an individual with a unique method. You'll receive five points for each hit. Of course, those points will be eliminated anytime you accidentally hit someone twice with the same method. So pay attention!

"The second column records every time you hit an individual with a fifth unique method. If you are hit five times by the same individual in five different methods, you will be eliminated from the game and your points will zero out. Eliminating someone from the game is worth five hundred points in that second column. The game runs for exactly one hour. Last person standing at the end of that hour wins the game. If there are multiple people still in play, the person with the most points wins."

Samantha stepped forward. "Now here's the part that's different for today's game, so pay attention. Serena and I will be acting as one unit, practicing our spells together. In order for us to be eliminated as a team, we both have to be hit by the same person five times."

"That means in order to eliminate one of us, you have to eliminate both of us." Serena said. "Of course, when you do, that will be worth a thousand points."

"In order to make things fair," Samantha said, "we're going to have all of you team up in pairs as well. Find your partner and then we'll be ready to begin."

Pandemonium ensued as the teens negotiated with each other, but eventually everyone had a partner. Jack and Neil, unsurprisingly, joined forces themselves, no doubt planning how to torment the twins throughout the game.

"All right," Samantha said. "Once you're inside the game, spread out and find an area for you and your partner to defend. Once everyone is in place, you will have five minutes to strategize before the game begins. When the buzzer goes off, you're free to cast your spells. No spell-casting until then. Understood?"

Heads nodded in response.

"Excellent. Head on in then. Best of luck to you all!"

With that, everyone bolted through the doors into the cavernous room made to resemble a town in the Old West.

Serena and Samantha made a beeline for a giant boulder at one end of the town. As they ran, Serena took note of where Jack and Neil headed (the town jail) and where several of the teens headed (some behind other boulders and others into the grocer's and the saloon).

"We need really good spells," Serena said as they collapsed behind the boulder.

"Agreed," Samantha said. "And we should totally think outside the box. They'll expect us to do the usual stuff. Paint, glitter, that kind of thing."

"But when have we ever been predictable?" Serena asked.

"Never," they both said together and giggled.

"I have a great idea," Samantha said, then set Serena off to giggling as she explained what she was thinking. Samantha's idea gave Serena one, and then another, and before they knew it, they had their first spell cast, just waiting for the buzzer to launch it, and several other spells waiting in the wings.

When the buzzer sounded, the twins launched from behind their boulder with a resounding war cry and started firing arrows left and right.

"What the hell, Serena?" Neil exclaimed from off to their left even as Jack bellowed from the right and several of the teens let out shrieks of surprise. "I think she just tagged me with a cowbell!"

The twins collapsed in giggles behind their boulder as the ringing of bells came from multiple directions.

"They won't be able to sneak up on us now," Serena giggled.

"Next spell?" Samantha asked.

"Next spell."

What followed was complete and utter chaos.

And so much fun.

Serena hadn't had this much fun with Samantha since they were kids.

Their second spell knotted the shoelaces of partners together, causing Neil and Jack utter frustration as they could barely hobble from one place to the next and had to hold onto each other for support.

Samantha and Serena almost got tagged by the kids, they were laughing so hard and focused on getting hilarious pictures of their men holding onto each other.

When the men decided they'd had enough and removed their shoes, the system called them out for cheating. "One hundred points deducted from Jack and Neil's score due to cheating," a robotic sounding voice announced, causing a huge amount of cursing from the men and hilarity from the teens and the twins.

The third spell the twins cast wasn't that bad at first as everyone they hit with their arrows received a mustache.

Jonathan and Max were their first victims. They were so proud to have suddenly grown mustaches, they got hit by a couple spells from Bianca and Jasmine because they were busy taking selfies on their phones.

It was only later, when the twins were starting to wonder if maybe that last spell hadn't worked, that Jonathan started shouting about his lip being on fire and Max demanded to know why his nose was itching.

Five minutes later, Jack and Neil were in the same boat.

The girls had clearly decided to steer clear of Serena and Samantha's boulder because they'd not managed to tag any of them as of yet.

"Just goes to prove that women are so much smarter than men," Serena said to Samantha, causing her to erupt in giggles. "You know our men are just going to double-down."

"Of course, they are," Samantha said. She peeked out around the boulder. "I think Kyle and Logan are determined to get revenge for Max and Jonathan, so get ready."

Serena grinned. This was just so much fun!

They managed to hit both Kyle and Logan with the itchy moustache spell and then followed it up with their fourth spell, which was so funny, they almost fell over themselves giggling and laughing.

Of course, Kyle and Logan managed to hit them both with a paint spell, but it was totally worth it.

Each of the boys now had a temporary tattoo on their foreheads that said, "Spell-Tagged by Serena and Samantha."

"Oh, that's not right!" Logan shouted when he caught sight of Kyle's tattoo, causing the twins to dissolve in laughter again.

At that moment, Jack and Neil popped around either side of their boulder and shot the twins, covering the two in glitter.

"Ugh," Serena groaned, shaking her head to dislodge glitter even as she shot Neil with the tattoo spell. "This will never come out."

He grinned, leaned over and kissed her, which completely blew all thoughts of the game from her head, then pulled back and shot her *again!*

"Hey!" She shouted as he laughed and backpedalled, calling, "All's fair in war, love!"

She turned to Samantha who was clearly in the same shape, looking a bit dazed. She also had a heart tattoo on her cheek with Jack's name in the center.

Samantha began to giggle.

"Mine says Neil, doesn't it?" Serena sighed.

"They think they're so clever," Samantha said. "I doubt they've been hitting the teens with that spell."

"I think we need to up our spell-game," Serena said.

"Reserve spell?" Samantha asked.

"Reserve spell." Serena agreed. They cast their carriers, pulled an arrow, popped up from the boulder and fired at their men, who disappeared into the jail at the last second.

The arrows disintegrated on impact with the door to the jail.

"Damn," Serena said.

"We'll just have to sneak up on them," Samantha said. "Ready?"

Serena peeked around the corner of her boulder. She didn't see any of the teens, but could hear them shouting. "I think the kids are all on the other side of the town, trying to get each other. We should be fine."

"Awesome. Let's go!"

The two women jumped up and raced toward the jail. They slid in under the jail's window, both of them now sporting a second splatter of paint, this time from Jack and Neil's arrows.

"We're still in much better shape than them," Serena said.

"Worth it," Samantha agreed. "On the count of three."

"One-Two-Three!" They both surged up onto their knees and aimed their arrows through the window at the men inside. Unfortunately, the men were ready for that and grabbed the arrows by the shaft, jerking them from the twins' hands.

"Hey!" Serena exclaimed.

Samantha was too busy laughing to speak.

The twins pulled several new arrows out of their carriers.

Serena pointed to the door and Samantha nodded.

They crawled their way to the door, counted to three silently, then barged in and started firing arrows left and right.

The minute Serena saw one of her arrows connect with Neil, she dived out of the jail, Samantha at her side. They crawled to either side of the door, then bolted to their feet and ran like the wind.

"Jack and Neil have been eliminated from the game," the automated voice announced, prompting cheers from the teens, even as a round of gagging and cursing erupted from the jail.

Serena and Samantha collapsed behind their boulder, safe once more and took stock.

"I think Jack hit me twice inside the jail," Samantha reported.

"I think Neil got me twice too," Serena said. "Good thing we got them back because I'm pretty sure the results of their spells wouldn't have been pretty."

The twins grinned at each other.

"I'm not sure Neil will ever forgive you," Samantha said.

"What about Jack?" Serena demanded.

"Eh, he adores me," Samantha said.

"Not enough for this, you aggravating wench," Jack growled as he stalked around the boulder, causing Samantha to let out a squeak of surprise.

"I may be eliminated from this game, Serena, but that doesn't mean I won't get my revenge," Neil said as he came around the boulder on her side.

The women took one look at the men and burst into laughter.

Their hair was now completely black with one white streak down the middle.

"Wait! What are you doing?" Samantha squealed. "Stay away. Don't get too close!"

Serena burst into laughter as Jack swept Samantha into his arms and buried his face in her neck, causing her to squeal and gag, but Serena's laughter died when Neal did the same to her.

"Ooh, no, Neil!"

"What's the matter, love? Not appreciating stench of skunk?"

Serena giggled even as she gagged. "Oh, goddess, stop, stop. I'll end the spell. I'll take it back. I promise!"

Chapter Eleven

SERENA WAS STILL smiling the next morning when she dragged Neil to an animal shelter to adopt some kittens.

Neil was driving, which meant she could spend the time reliving memories from the day before.

It had truly been a perfect day, from waking in Neil's arms to tumbling into bed with him at the end of it. The fun they'd had at the center had just been the icing on top.

She couldn't remember the last time she'd laughed so hard and it was even better that she'd shared those moments with her sister and with Neil.

She'd well and truly fallen in love with him and somehow, around the same time, had gotten her best friend, her sister, back.

It had been years since she and Samantha had tried casting spells together and yesterday was the first time they'd experienced real success in the process.

She wasn't sure if it was because they were more relaxed in a setting without pressure, or if it was because they were both in love and therefore, happy, or if it was simply that they were older and more in control. Whatever the reason, though (and she absolutely refused to believe it was because of their mother's ridiculous spells), she was so very grateful and couldn't wait to play at the center with her sister again.

They were planning to make it a regular occurrence as it would be good practice, not just for them, but for the teens as well. Plus it was just fantastic fun.

"So how's the article coming along?" She asked Neil.

"Almost finished. You can read the final draft later today."

"Cool." Serena hesitated, but then blurted out, "So does that mean you won't be needing to come to the center anymore?"

Neil chuckled. "Do you really think I've been coming to the center just for the story? I had most everything I needed several days ago."

Serena smiled. "Well, I didn't know, now did I?"

Neil pulled into the animal rescue parking lot, then turned and kissed her. "I promise. There are much better reasons than my job for me to spend time at the center. The teens are worth my time and so are you."

Serena flung her arms around his neck and kissed him. Just as it was getting fantastically hot, she pulled away. "Let's go get us some kittens, shall we?"

She hopped out of the car and met Neil on the sidewalk.

"You did that on purpose," he grumbled as he grabbed her hand and pulled her toward the rescue's door. "Don't worry. I'll get my revenge later."

Serena giggled.

* * *

Neil was so in love, it wasn't even funny.

He couldn't take his eyes off Serena, who was sitting on the floor in a room filled with cages, crooning and cuddling two enormous, black cats.

"I thought you wanted kittens," he said.

"Yes, but look at them. They belong with us, don't you think?"

Neil rolled his eyes. "Why? Because they're black? Are you seriously buying into that ridiculous stereotype about witches and black cats?"

"Of course not, but I *am* buying into the very real statistic that black cats have a terrible time being adopted and these two aren't kittens anymore, so it'll be even harder for them. Right?" She looked up at the rescue worker, who nodded in agreement.

Neil smiled. "Well, they are adorable and they clearly love you."

Serena beamed up at him. "I love them already. What are their names?"

"Not a clue," Neil said.

Serena scowled at him. "Not you, doofus."

"Inky and Boo," the rescue worker said.

"Oh, how adorable!"

After cuddling the cats one final time, Serena filled out the adoption paperwork, made arrangements to pick up the cats later that morning, then dragged Neil to the Pet Emporium to get some cat necessities.

When she was captivated by a huge cat tree, one even larger than the one Samantha had purchased for her kittens, Neil tried to convince Serena that one so large wasn't necessary.

"Are you suggesting that I deprive my cats of a tree as luxurious as the one Samantha provided her kittens?" Serena demanded, hands on hips.

Neil laughed. "I wouldn't dream of suggesting such a thing." He swept her into a heated kiss, then called Jack for help transporting the monstrosity.

* * *

Serena had so much fun once they got back to her place with the cats and their many accessories. She drove Neil crazy, moving the cat tree from spot to spot until she found the perfect place for it.

It was his own fault for insisting on moving it for her each time. She kept offering to move it herself, but he insisted, though he definitely didn't appreciate it when she told him she thought she wanted it back in its original spot.

She burst into laughter at the look on his face. "I'm kidding, I'm kidding. It's perfect right here."

"Are you sure?"

"Positive." She kissed him, and of course, one thing led to another, and it wasn't until much later that she was able to check on the cats again.

When she did, she found them stretched out on the cat tree in patches of sunlight, proving she'd chosen exactly the right spot after all.

Serena and Neil spent the rest of the day doing the same things over and over again: playing with the cats, then taking breaks to play with each other, then seeking out the cats again to make sure they were doing fine (they always were).

After a full day of doing nothing but playing with cats and each other, they retired early to while away the hours, thumping thighs, banging the headboard and every other euphemism Serena could think of, and when they were perfectly satiated, they lay in each other's arms and talked long into the night.

Serena shared that she and Samantha were meeting for breakfast the next day to come up with a plan for how to deal with their interfering mother.

"I mean, it's not like we can really complain, since it's entirely possible (though I'll never admit it to her) that her spell is the reason we're together."

"Doubtful," Neil said.

"Well, it's definitely the reason Samantha and Jack are together. Samantha was *never* going to go there, but then Mother cast that spell and the rest was history."

Neil chuckled. "You and I have been dancing around each other for years. So have Jack and Samantha. I have no doubt they would have eventually found their way together, just as we would have, with or without your mother's spell."

"You're probably right. The question is whether we would have been ninety when it happened."

Neil laughed. "Okay, fine. Maybe we owe your mother a tiny bit of gratitude, but if you offer it to her—"

"She'll be unbearable, I know. Plus she'll take it as permission to interfere in our lives again, which is why Serena and I will be brainstorming a solution in the morning."

"Well, based on how the two of you trounced Jack and I at Spell-Tag yesterday, I'd say your mother'd better take cover."

Serena giggled. "You know it!"

* * *

Serena and Neil parted ways outside her house the next morning.

He had an early morning meeting at the newsroom and she had her morning breakfast with Serena.

"Good luck with your mother," he murmured against her lips.

"Thanks," she whispered, then kissed him for about the seventeen hundredth time that morning. "See you tonight."

By the time she got to the cafe where she was meeting her sister, her thoughts were centered on the upcoming battle.

"You know she'll be absolutely intolerable," Samantha groaned the instant Serena's butt hit her chair.

Jack, who had been keeping Samantha company until Serena arrived, chuckled. "I'll leave you two alone so you can come up with a game plan." He kissed Samantha, then headed out.

The twins watched as he jogged across the street and into their work building.

They both sighed at the same time, then glanced at each other and burst into laughter.

"Seriously," Samantha said. "How did I ever get so lucky?"

"How did *we* get so lucky?" Serena corrected.

Samantha grinned. "That's right. You and Neil were looking pretty cozy on Saturday."

"I can't believe it, but I think I'm in love," Serena said.

"I'm so happy for you, sis. I really am. I'm just not loving how Mother's going to react to this bit of news. She's already insufferable because of me and Jack."

Serena grinned. "I know, but I've been thinking about it and I think I've come up with a foolproof plan."

"Oh, good."

"I'm thinking we need to come up with something utterly reckless for you to do."

"But I don't want to be reckless," Samantha wailed.

"Something she would absolutely hate."

"But, *Serena*, I don't *want* to be reckless."

"I know, I know, but hear me out. Something reckless for you and something utterly restrained for me. Something she'd hate for both of us. We're not going to *do* whatever it is, of course. The point is to make her *think* her spell has backfired in a horrific way."

"Ooooh, this has a lot of potential," Serena exclaimed. "I know! Jack and I can move to Africa."

"Not bad. You need a reason why though."

"Um. Because we're looking for adventure?"

"Perfect! Especially because she'd have no one to blame but herself. After all, she cursed you with recklessness, and we all know that recklessness is in the eye of the beholder. In my eye, it's code for adventurous."

Samantha giggled. "She's going to *hate* this. What about you?"

"I think I'm going to have to quit my job and go back to school to get my PhD in …" Serena paused. "… in what?"

"Nothing that will benefit the business," Samantha said.

"Okay, so… education? Oooh, I'm going to be a high school English teacher. Perfect."

They both giggled.

"I can't wait to see her face," Samantha said.

They spent the next twenty minutes hammering out the details, then another forty grilling each other about their love lives.

It was truly another perfect moment in Serena's life, bonding with her sister over their newfound happiness.

Later that morning, at exactly ten-fifteen, Serena walked into her mother's office just in time to hear Elizabeth wail, "Africa?"

It was all Serena could do not to bust out laughing. "Hey, Samantha, Jack. Sorry to interrupt. I just needed to give this to Mother."

Serena handed her letter to Elizabeth, who looked rather surprised, then turned and walked away.

She'd almost reached the door when Elizabeth barked, "Stop right there, young lady! What is the meaning of this?"

Serena turned around and raised an eyebrow. "I thought I was perfectly clear in the letter."

"You can't resign. Why are you resigning?"

"You ready, Serena?"

She turned, surprised to see Neil standing in the door. "What are you doing here?"

He grinned. "I thought I'd come and see you off. After all, it's not every day a woman goes off to college to become a teacher."

"A teacher? Serena?" Elizabeth exclaimed.

"Why are you so surprised, Mother?" Serena asked. She turned and walked back toward her mother, pausing so that she stood shoulder-to-shoulder with Samantha, Neil a solid presence at her back. "It's a perfectly reasonable occupation."

"Yes, but—" Elizabeth's eyes narrowed. "Are you two having me on?"

"Why whatever do you mean, Mother?" Samantha asked. "You did want me to be a bit more adventurous, right? I thought you'd be happy to hear we're off to Africa."

"I'm quite looking forward to it," Jack said. "When we're finished with Africa, perhaps we could explore Asia."

"Oooh, and Antarctica!" Samantha squealed. "I've always wanted to see the penguins."

"Oh, now I *know* you're having me on," Elizabeth said.

"Personally, I'm looking forward to working with teens every day," Serena said. "The volunteering I've been doing at the center has really prepared me for this new career, I think."

"Come on, now, girls," Elizabeth said. "Please tell me you're joking."

Serena waved a hand at the letter her mother was holding. "Would I joke about something as serious as going back to school?"

"But the spells weren't even real!" Elizabeth wailed.

"What?" Serena and Samantha chorused at the same time.

"Do you really think I would risk you doing something utterly reckless right before the fundraising event, Samantha?"

"Well—" Samantha began, but Elizabeth cut her off.

"And do you honestly think I'd want you to restrain your outside-the-box thinking when it benefits the company and the center so much, Serena?"

"I—" Serena shook her head. "What exactly are you saying?" She was so confused.

"*There was no spell.* I just zapped the two of you with a bit of my power. That's all."

Jack let out a bark of laughter. "So let me get this straight. Samantha running late, rescuing kittens—"

"Hanging out in broom closets," Serena inserted.

"Serena!" Samantha glared at her.

Serena grinned and gave a shrug. "Just saying."

"Well then, I'll add to the list," Samantha snapped. "Serena showing up early, going home all alone the night of the event—"

"—driving like a little old lady," Neil said dryly.

"Hey!" Serena exclaimed, sending an elbow back into his gut. He just chuckled, a delicious sound that made her shiver.

"So all of that was what exactly, if not the result of a spell?" Jack asked.

Elizabeth shrugged. "That was just the twins making choices in their everyday lives, the way we all do. None of it was influenced by a spell."

"So what was the point of pretending then?" Samantha exclaimed.

"The point was to give the two of you a bit of freedom, so that you could act in a way contrary to what's always been expected of you. And look at the result!" She waved a hand at the four of them. "You've both found love."

"Yes, I'd say your plan worked perfectly," Serena said. "Samantha's off to Africa in search of adventure, thanks to you, Mother, and I'm going to be a teacher, so job well-done."

"Yes, but there was no spell," Elizabeth repeated, "so there's no *reason* for you two to be making these crazy choices."

No reason? The fact their mother had been manipulating them from minute one was reason enough, as far as Serena was concerned, which was why she wouldn't be letting their mother off the hook anytime soon.

"I don't think moving to Africa's crazy, do you, Jack?" Samantha asked.

"Not at all," he said. "It's fun and adventurous."

"Exactly!"

"And okay, the salary isn't the greatest, but I don't think teaching qualifies as crazy either, Mother," Serena said. "Besides, I'm looking forward to teaching young minds the benefits of iambic pentameter and how poetry can be used as a focal point when spell-casting." She avoided looking at anyone in the room but her mother. If she caught anyone else's eyes, she'd surely ruin everything by laughing.

"Iambic pentameter?" Elizabeth demanded.

Serena heard a snort from her left. She wasn't sure if it was Samantha or Jack, but knew it couldn't be Neil since he was still standing behind her, driving her crazy with one broad hand on her hip, the other playing with the curls at the nape of her neck.

"You can iambic pentameter me anytime you like," he murmured in her ear, making her shiver with delight.

How did he *do* that? Make something as innocent as a poetic device sound dirty?

She turned, grabbed Neil's hand and started pulling him toward the door. "And on that note, we'll be in my office if anyone needs anything." She stopped at the door and glanced back. "Nobody'd better need anything though." She gave a jaunty grin and sauntered out, Neil at her heels.

She heard Jack and Samantha laughing behind them, and figured they'd clue their mother in at some point, but even if they didn't, Elizabeth would eventually figure things out when Samantha and Jack never left for Africa and Serena failed to enroll in a teaching program.

Serena didn't really care though because Neil had her engines revved high. It was time to take care of some other business.

She pulled him into her office, slammed the door and shoved him up against it. "I can't believe you left work to come here."

He grinned. "Are you kidding me? Once you sent me that text, there was no way I was going to miss the fireworks. Glad I made it in time."

She kissed him until they were both drowning in the heat of their passion, then pulled back to ask, "You ready to iambic pentameter me?"

"Oh, darlin'. I was born ready."

Discover more stories by Pepper

at www.peppermcgraw.com

Other Books by Pepper

MURRYSVILLE COALITION
The Crazy Cheetah Lady
One Sad Kitty

A PAWSITIVELY PURRFECT MATCH
Catnapped
The Real McCat
Unbearably Cute

SHENANIGANS ANTHOLOGIES
Crazed
Amazed
Holidazed

STORIES OF THE VEIL
Guardians of the Veil
The Unveiled
The Veiled

About the Author

Pepper would love to be able to shift into an animal (any animal, really, though she's rather partial to cats). Unfortunately, since she wasn't lucky enough to be born a shifter, she's had to settle for writing about them instead.

She's an advocate of animal rescue and supports local shelters and Trap-Neuter-Release programs for feral cats. She's had the supreme honor of winning occasional head butts and meows from the local ferals in her neighborhood and even of convincing a few to come inside and adopt her as their own.

You can find out more about Pepper's books on her website www.peppermcgraw.com or on social media @peppermcgraw.

www.ingramcontent.com/pod-product-compliance
Lightning Source LLC
Chambersburg PA
CBHW071253190726
48292CB00007B/2517